AMISH MURDER

ETTIE SMITH AMISH MYSTERIES BOOK 2

SAMANTHA PRICE

CHAPTER 1

"She must've made someone angry. Not many people get killed by staying in their own homes and minding their own business," Ettie said to her sister, Elsa-May.

Elsa-May looked at her over the top of her glasses. "Who? Camille Esh?"

Ettie frowned. "How many other women do we know who've been murdered recently?"

"I was only half-listening. *Jah*, you're right about that. People do get murdered in their own homes, but usually by more violent means."

Ettie dropped her sampler into her lap. "She must've known the person who killed her. They must have slipped the poison into her food; maybe even when she was in her apartment, which means she might even have entertained her killer."

Elsa-May shivered and then shook her head.

"What is it?" Ettie asked.

"The whole thing's awful, and anyway, who would've wanted her dead?"

"You didn't know her as well as I did. There was more to that girl than first met the eye. She could've stepped on some toes when she left our community."

Elsa-May continued knitting at a slower pace than usual. They'd just finished cleaning up after breakfast and had settled in for a quiet day. "I'd say you're right. I know Camille's stepmother, Mildred, always had a rough time with her. The two never got along. How is Camille's *bruder* Jacob now? I haven't seen Mildred or Jacob since Camille's funeral."

"Jacob's coping, but Mildred's missing her husband. Nehemiah wasn't even that old."

"Much younger than both of us," Ettie added. "And it was a shock that Nehemiah died, and just weeks later, Camille was murdered."

Elsa-May glanced down at her knitting and then looked back up at Ettie, not missing a stitch of the intricate pattern she'd learned by heart. "I've been meaning to ask you, have you thought about what you're going to do with the *haus?*"

Ettie had recently been left a house by her dear friend, Agatha.

"I would sell, except Agatha wanted her young friend, Ava, to stay in the *grossdaddi haus* forever – for as long as she wanted." Ettie placed her needlework in her lap again and looked across the small living room at her older sister. "That's my only sticking point. I'll have to keep the *haus* longer for that very reason. In the meantime, I'll have

Jeremiah, your favorite grandson, do some work on the house for me."

Elsa-May chuckled. "You can't say he's my favorite, Ettie. I don't have any favorites."

"The first *grosskinner* always holds a special place, and don't even try to tell me otherwise."

Elsa-May shook her head at her sister and remained silent.

Ettie kept talking. "He's such a *gut* builder. Not only that, he's so handy with other odd jobs. I don't think I could live in the *haus,* though. I'd forever be thinking about Horace being killed and hidden under the floorboards for so many years."

Ettie had been turned off the idea of living in the house. She'd been happy when she found out Agatha had willed her the house, but when Jeremiah found Agatha's old beau, Horace, buried under the floor, the discovery brought with it a disturbing chain of events.

Elsa-May nodded. "That's good. I don't think you'd get the best money for the *haus* the way that it is."

"Remind me to go there tomorrow and have a look so I can make a list of everything that needs doing. I'll see your Jeremiah on Sunday, and ask him to come out and give me a quote." Ettie looked at her sister's smiling face. "Are you happy I'm staying on here in the *haus* with you?"

The corners of Elsa-May's mouth suddenly turned downward. "Please yourself."

Ettie frowned at her. She knew Elsa-May would have missed her if she had moved to Agatha's old house. Why was it so hard for Elsa-May to admit it?

With the exception of the loud tick of the old wooden

clock that hung on the wall, the next moments were silent.

Ettie finally spoke. "We should have Jeremiah and Ava over for dinner again. If the two of them got married that would solve my problem of her living in the *grossdaddi haus.*"

Elsa-May chortled and pushed her glasses further up her nose. "Unless Jeremiah moves into it too."

"*Jah*, I hadn't thought of that. It might be best if I lease the main house out, then I'd have no worries."

"That sounds a reasonable solution." Elsa-May continued knitting, moving her elevated sore leg slightly.

Elsa-May and Ettie spent a great deal of their time in their living room with Elsa-May knitting and Ettie concentrating on her needlework.

The sisters stared at each other when a loud knock broke through the silence.

"Who could that be?" Elsa-May asked.

"I didn't hear a buggy. I'll go see." Ettie placed her needlework on the chair next to her and hurried to open the door. They rarely got visitors who walked to their house, and the neighbors, although they were close, mostly kept to themselves. When Ettie swung the door open, she was faced with a stern-faced Detective Kelly. She frowned at him, wondering if she'd done something wrong. Detective Kelly had never been as nice to them as Detective Crowley. There was something about Detective Kelly that Ettie wasn't comfortable with.

"Good morning, Mrs. Smith. May I come in for a moment or two?"

"Good morning, Detective. Certainly." She stepped aside to give him room to move through. "Come in."

"Thank you." Two strides further and he was in the living room of the small home. "Good morning," he said to Elsa-May with a nod.

"Morning. Have a seat, Detective," Elsa-May said, still sitting.

Once the detective sat down, he rocked a little on his chair. "It's not going to break, is it?"

Elsa-May smiled. "I don't think so. I'll have my grandson, Jeremiah, take a look at it."

"Yes, good idea. I know Jeremiah. I met him before at Mrs. Smith's other house."

"We were just talking about the whole business with Horace." Before Ettie took a seat, she asked, "Would you like some hot tea, and cake?" He shook his head, and sat down on a creaky wooden chair.

Ettie sat down on their only couch while she waited to hear why he was there.

He looked from one to the other. "I'm hoping you ladies might be able to help me."

The sisters glanced at each other with raised eyebrows. Just a few months back he'd warned Ettie to keep out of his way. He sure hadn't wanted their help back then.

Elsa-May leaned forward. "Regarding what?"

Ettie had an idea why he was there. The only reason could be that he wanted their help over the recent murder of Camille Esh.

Detective Kelly rubbed his lined forehead and said, "Do you know Jacob Esh and his family?"

"You're here about Camille?" Elsa-May asked.

He nodded. "We have reason to believe that her brother might have killed her."

Elsa-May shook her head. "That's nonsense!"

"We've got reason to believe that..."

"What would possibly give you reason to believe anything of the kind?" Ettie interrupted the detective. She was outraged he could think such a thing.

He held his hands up. "I'm not here to argue back and forth. I'm here because I need your help. Before I go any further, I need to tell you that I do believe the man's innocent. No one in your community will talk to me, so there's my problem right there. I need some of you Amish people to answer my questions. I've been ignored completely – others have shut themselves in their houses and refused to come to the door."

"What would you like us to do?" Ettie asked. "We can't make them speak to you."

"I'd like you to find out a few things for me. That's all! It'll have to be 'off the record', of course. But once I know what's happened, then I'll be in a position where I can help Jacob."

"We'll do whatever we can to help him," Ettie said.

Elsa-May nodded enthusiastically.

The detective leaned so far over that he placed his elbows on his knees. "If we don't find out what happened soon, Jacob could go to jail for a long time, or worse." He straightened up. "Tell me, what do you know about Jacob and the relationship he had with his sister?"

The elderly sisters started talking at the same time, then stopped and looked at each other.

"You go first, Ettie."

Ettie smiled, and then turned to the detective. "Jacob and Camille left the community as soon as they could. Jacob…"

"Jacob left when he was eighteen, I believe, and then two years later, Camille followed when she was around the same age."

Ettie turned and stared at her sister. "You told me to go first."

"So they were both out of the community for a good twenty years?" the detective asked.

"My goodness, is Jacob around forty now?" Elsa-May asked.

The detective nodded. "He is, and his sister was two years younger than he is."

Ettie was quick to answer before Elsa-May butted in again. "To answer your question correctly, Detective, she came back to the community around two years ago. I'm a good friend of Camille's stepmother, Mildred. Poor Mildred – Camille never liked her right from the start. Anyone would think a young girl would be pleased to have a stepmother after her mother died. Surely it would be better than no mother at all. Nehemiah married Mildred two years after Mary's death. Camille was five at the time."

"Mildred was Camille's stepmother, then?" the detective asked.

"Yes." Ettie answered.

"The detective doesn't need to know all that, Ettie."

Kelly looked at Elsa-May. "Actually, it might be helpful." He looked back at Ettie. "Camille didn't get along with Mildred when she was five years old? I would've thought that a child that young would've adjusted better than that."

"To everyone on the outside it appeared that way, but Mildred told me what had gone on behind closed doors. It would surprise even you, Detective. She was a very different girl when no one was watching."

The lines in Kelly's forehead deepened. "Go on."

Ettie rubbed her neck. "I feel terrible. Mildred told me these things in confidence."

Elsa-May frowned. "What things?"

"Anything you tell me could help Jacob," the detective said. He nodded, urging her to continue.

"To put it bluntly, then, the girl used to do dreadful things at home and make it look like Mildred did them. She did everything she could to turn her father against Mildred. She broke Mary's china clock, which Nehemiah had given her on their wedding day. Mary was Camille's mother. It was a beautiful thing with tiny pink rosebuds the entire way around the face of the clock."

"Get to the point, Ettie," her sister said.

Ettie glanced at Elsa-May then looked back at the detective. "When Nehemiah got home that night, Camille told him that Mildred broke it in a fit of temper. He didn't think for one moment that Camille might have broken her mother's clock."

"You never told me about all of that," Elsa-May said.

Ettie nodded. "Camille did things like that all the time. At first, Nehemiah believed Camille, and I believe it caused a rift in Nehemiah and Mildred's marriage in the early days. Then one day, when he overheard Camille talking to Mildred, he knew Camille had been lying about everything."

"Children do go through stages and she was dreadfully upset about her mother's death," Elsa-May said.

"I know that," Ettie said. "And Mildred and Nehemiah tried to be understanding, but she never got along with Mildred. Ever."

"Did Jacob get along with Mildred?" the detective asked.

"Oh, yes, but Jacob and Camille never got along. Not as far back as I can remember. The pair were always at odds with one another, but that doesn't mean he'd kill her."

"Of course, a great many siblings don't care for each other," Detective Kelly said.

Elsa-May said, "I remember they were always competitive, each telling the other they could do better at any given task. I remember, years back, one day at one of the softball games…"

"The detective doesn't need to know that, Elsa-May." Ettie was pleased to mirror Elsa-May's former comment right back at her.

Elsa-May narrowed her eyes at Ettie.

"I do, if it's relevant," the detective said.

"It's not," Ettie said abruptly, making sure to avoid Elsa-May's stern gaze.

The detective looked at Elsa-May, raised his eyebrows, and then turned back to Ettie. "What about Camille's more recent history?"

"As I said, she'd left the community many years ago, and

then once Nehemiah had started getting frail, Camille came back to run the farm. She told him she had business experience, so Nehemiah handed things over to her. He really had no choice with Jacob gone. Normally sons take over from the father, but with Jacob not in the community Nehemiah handed the running of the farm over to Camille."

"So when did Jacob come back to the farm?" the detective asked, tipping his head slightly to one side.

Elsa-May said, "Camille came back two years ago, like Ettie already told you. Jacob returned around six months ago. So I imagine in those last few months the siblings both tried to run the farm together. As you probably know already, Camille and Jacob's father died only weeks before Camille was killed."

Ettie continued, "The two were still at odds with one another, just like when they were younger, according to Mildred. When I say 'the two', I mean Camille and Jacob. I think Mildred was used to the fact that Camille was never going to like or accept her into the family. It was hard for Mildred, especially since she never had children of her own."

"Camille was murdered in the apartment she'd moved into, so we know that she'd left the community again by then," the detective said.

"Camille left after Nehemiah died," Ettie said.

The detective repositioned himself in his chair. "What do you mean?"

Ettie took a deep breath, waiting for Elsa-May to jump in and speak for her as she normally did whenever she hesitated. Ettie frowned at Elsa-May when she made no attempt to speak, and continued, "Each thought they knew how to run the farm better. Nehemiah wasn't happy with how Camille had done certain things and he complained to Jacob. Nehemiah let Camille know that she was no longer running the farm and gave the job to Jacob."

The detective sighed. "No, I wasn't asking about that. I want to know why Camille left after Nehemiah died."

"Well, that's what I'm trying to tell you – this is how it happened. Jacob stayed and Camille left. In the will, the farm was left solely to Jacob."

Now Elsa-May interrupted, "So, she had no reason to stick around. Nehemiah was pleased to have his son back before he died. Wasn't he, Ettie?"

Ettie nodded. "Yes, he was pleased that Jacob came back to run the farm. After that, Camille had even more reason to resent poor old Jacob." Seeing the detective open his mouth to speak, Ettie added, "Jacob would never hurt a fly."

After Detective Kelly took a deep breath, he said, "That's my next question. Did Jacob ever show signs of violence or anger toward anyone?"

Both Elsa-May and Ettie shook their heads.

Ettie said, "Not while he was a part of our community. I believe he hasn't got a mean bone in his body."

"But you both wouldn't know him very well if he left when he was eighteen and he only came back to the community recently," Detective Kelly said, looking pleased with himself.

"I believe a person's personality is formed very early in life. Jacob was always a kind boy in his youth." Before the detective could speak again, Elsa-May quickly added, "You said you thought there was some kind of proof that Jacob killed Camille, so what do you have that you're calling 'proof'?"

"No, Elsa-May, I believe the detective's words were that he 'had reason to believe' that Jacob might have killed Camille. He never said anything about having proof." Ettie turned to Kelly. "Isn't that right, Detective?"

"That's correct, Mrs. Smith; that's exactly what I said. We don't have proof, as such, but what we do have is someone who's willing to testify that Camille told her that she suspected Jacob was trying to kill her."

"Utter rubbish," Elsa-May blurted out.

The detective whipped his head around toward Elsa-May. "Are you certain?"

"Yes, why would he kill his own sister? Besides, Jacob's the one who inherited the farm. There was no reason for him to kill her – no monetary reason."

The detective looked between the two of them. "According to the both of you, they didn't get along. A lifetime of not getting along with someone could be the only reason he needed. It's not uncommon for a perfectly sane person to kill another in a fit of rage. It happens every day. Most often people are murdered by someone close to them, such as a spouse, or a family member."

"You did say you thought he was innocent, Detective?" Ettie asked.

"Yes, and I'd like you ladies to help me prove that. I've got pressure on me to solve this case. I'm up for a promotion, and it wouldn't hurt if I could wrap this one up quickly."

Elsa-May huffed. "You didn't want Ettie's help when she tried to help with Horace's murder."

The detective turned to Ettie. "This time, Mrs. Smith, I'd be grateful for your help." He looked at Elsa-May. "And yours too, of course."

"I'm afraid it'll just be Ettie. With my sore leg, I can't do anything. I can't walk very far." Elsa-May rubbed the top of her leg.

"Nothing serious, I hope."

"No, just a niggle."

The detective tilted his head to one side. "A niggle?"

Elsa-May chuckled. "Something that's annoying."

"I'll be glad to help you prove that Jacob is innocent, Detective," Ettie said.

"People will talk to Ettie," Elsa-May said.

"That's what I'm banking on." The detective looked back at Ettie. "When none of your people would talk to me, naturally I thought of you ladies."

Elsa-May asked, "Do you have any leads at all on the murderer?"

Kelly rubbed his nose. "No. We're still waiting for forensic results to come back. I do have a statement from that woman Camille spoke with."

Elsa-May laughed. "You had me worried for a minute. I thought you were about to lock Jacob away."

Ettie noticed the detective swallowed rather hard at Elsa-May's comment, which made her wonder if he was keeping something from them. Did he have some evidence he didn't want to share with them? He did look kind of guilty at that moment.

The detective rose to his feet. "Can I leave it to you

ladies to see what you can find out?" He looked at Ettie. "I guess it'll be just you asking around?"

Ettie pushed herself up from the couch. "I'll do that for you, but you're leaving me in the dark. What exactly do you want me to find out?"

"I need to know what the exact situation was between brother and sister. Did Jacob have any motive in the slightest to want Camille dead? For that matter, did anyone else have reason to want her gone?"

"I'll see what I can find out," Ettie said, walking the detective to the door.

"Goodbye," Elsa-May called out.

Before Kelly had a chance to say goodbye to Elsa-May, Ettie explained, "It hurts Elsa-May to stand with her bad leg."

"Yes, she mentioned that." The detective nodded goodbye to Elsa-May. He then turned to Ettie. "I do appreciate your help, Mrs. Smith. I know we haven't seen eye-to-eye before, but let's let bygones be bygones, shall we?"

"Of course, we can do that."

The detective stepped out the door and walked down the steps toward his car. Ettie watched him all the while.

CHAPTER 2

*W*hen Detective Kelly left, Ettie wasted no time in visiting Mildred. The last time she'd seen her was the day after Camille's funeral.

Just as Ettie knocked on the door, Mildred swung it open.

"Ettie, I'm so pleased you've come."

Ettie gave Mildred a quick hug before Mildred ushered her into the living room. "Can I get you something?"

"Nee denke. I've just had a visit from a detective." Ettie figured the straightforward approach would be best.

Mildred scowled. "About Camille?"

Ettie nodded. "Jah."

"Why did he go to you?"

"He knows me because I met him when poor Horace was found under Agatha's floor. Anyway, the detective thinks... Well, he's got some crazy notion that Jacob is involved somehow."

Mildred looked away from her. "Impossible." She

looked back at Ettie. "Why should we talk to him? Is that why you're here, to get us to speak to him?"

"Nee. I'm not here to ask you to do that. The truth of the matter is that he wants me to find out what I can about the whole thing." Ettie tapped her chin. "Would you talk to him?"

Mildred shook her head.

"Do you have any idea who might have done it?"

"Not at all. I mean, she didn't have many friends."

"You mean she had no friends?"

Mildred groaned. "Nee, she did have a couple of friends, but they were *Englischers*. She still kept in contact with two people. I never met them, but she'd receive letters from them, and I think she used to meet them in town. People would tell me they saw her speaking with *Englischers*."

"I might have a cup of hot tea," Ettie said.

"Come with me and we can talk while I make it."

Ettie followed Mildred into the kitchen. "I'm just glad that Nehemiah's not here. He'd never be able to get over Camille being murdered. Especially the way it happened."

Once Mildred put the pot on to boil, they both sat at the kitchen table.

Ettie asked, "From what you told me before, Camille and Jacob had an argument over Nehemiah's will?" That's something Ettie could have told the detective but didn't.

"Nehemiah didn't like the way Camille ran the farm. Among other things, we started losing money and we'd never lost money before. She never was good with finances and that's one of the reasons Nehemiah left the farm to Jacob. She had told her *vadder* she had management experience but it soon became clear she had none. Nehemiah had given her a good chance and she'd been running the farm for nearly two years before Jacob came back to us."

"*Jah*, you told me that before, about Camille not running the farm to Nehemiah's liking." Ettie raised her eyebrows. "Pardon me for asking, but the whole farm was left just to Jacob?"

Mildred nodded. "Nehemiah discussed it with me before he made the will. I said I didn't want a share. All I wanted was to live in the house here for the rest of my days. It makes sense since I was never blessed with *kinner*, and would never even have *kinskind* of my own." The corners of Mildred's mouth drooped.

Ettie couldn't imagine not having children or grandchildren. Although Ettie didn't see her own that often, they filled her life with a sense of purpose and wellbeing.

Mildred continued, "Better to leave everything to Camille and Jacob. Nehemiah knew that if he left the farm to Camille she'd see to it that I was put out on the street without anything to live on, and Nehemiah didn't want me to end up homeless when he was gone."

Ettie nodded, knowing that Jacob and Mildred had a bond like mother and son, and Jacob would look after her.

Mildred sighed. "After Nehemiah died, Camille found out she wasn't getting the farm and she and Jacob had some terrible rows. She carried on so badly that Jacob ended up offering her half the farm."

"That was generous of him."

"Camille didn't think so; she said she wanted the

whole farm. She accused him of only coming back to take the farm from her."

"What did she mean by that?"

"I suppose she meant that he knew his father was close to the end and he chose to return at that time only so he'd inherit the farm. You see, it wasn't until Nehemiah died that she found out she didn't get the farm; he didn't let her know beforehand that she wasn't going to get it. I suppose Nehemiah didn't want to be the victim of one of her outbursts. That girl had such a temper. When she found out that she didn't get the farm, she left the community and leased an apartment in town. She told Jacob she would see him in court."

"She did? You never told me she sued him."

"I don't think it came to anything. We never heard from a lawyer or anything. If she stayed here she might have been safe. She moved to that apartment and that's where they found her."

Ettie rubbed her chin. She hadn't liked to ask Mildred too many questions when she'd learned about Camille's death. Camille threatening to start legal proceedings might have given Jacob motive, but then again, he'd already offered her half the land. Surely a court wouldn't be more generous than Jacob had already been. Did she really expect the courts would award her the entire farm and leave her brother with nothing?

"I know what you're thinking, Ettie. It's like the story of the prodigal son returning."

"I wasn't thinking anything of the kind. Anyway, Camille and Jacob's situation was a little different since

Jacob inherited everything and Camille was left with nothing."

"Nee, I never said she got nothing."

Ettie tilted her head to one side. "What do you mean? Did she get left something?"

"Nee, but she did have a trust fund that Nehemiah set up for her when she was twenty five. He was concerned she wasn't married so he set up the fund. He had a lot of money in the bank and the man at the bank said he should do something with it. That's when he thought that Camille should have something, some kind of security."

"Did she have access to it?"

"I'm not certain about any of it. I do know that Nehemiah put Jacob in charge of the money."

"Jacob was the trustee?"

"Is that what you call it when someone can't get at the money unless the other person allows them?"

Ettie nodded, and then pulled a wry face. Jacob probably wasn't the best choice of a trustee since he and his sister had never gotten along. "And has Jacob inherited the money now that Camille's gone?"

"I'm not certain. Whenever Jacob tells me about business matters or money I just block my ears." Mildred covered her ears with the palms of her hands.

Another motive, if Jacob inherited the money from Camille's trust fund.

"Oh, the water's boiling." Mildred got up to pour the tea, and as she did so, something out the window caught her eye. She pulled the heavy curtain aside.

"What is it, Mildred?" Ettie asked, getting up to see what she was staring at.

"Just that pesky fellow from next door. He's been bothering Jacob to sell the farm, and before that, he was pestering Camille when he thought she might have had some say. He can't leave things well enough alone."

"He shouldn't be upsetting people like that." Ettie peeped out the window to see a stout man who appeared to be in his fifties, standing just beyond the property line. "He's an *Englischer?*"

"*Jah,* his name's Ronald Bradshaw."

"Why does he want the farm so badly?"

"I don't know."

"Has he told Jacob why he wants it?" Ettie asked.

"You'd have to ask Jacob about that. I'd dare say he wants to increase his own farm size, since land around these parts is getting scarce."

Ettie looked out again at the man who now had his hands on his hips gazing at the house. "What's he doing just standing there like that?"

"Beats me. He's probably putting a hex on the place or something, since we won't sell."

Ettie giggled. "Have you ever spoken to the man yourself?"

"*Nee.* He's never come to the door. He's spoken to Jacob when he was out in the fields." Mildred moved away from the window and continued making the tea.

After taking one last look at the man, Ettie sat back down at the table. Mildred placed a cup of tea in front of Ettie and then sat down next to her.

Ronald Bradshaw had to live on the farm with the white house and the red roof, Ettie figured. They were the only *Englischers* that had a property neighboring the Eshes' farm.

Once Ettie took a sip of tea, she placed the cup back on the saucer and looked directly at Mildred. "Do you have any idea who might have killed Camille?"

With a slight raise of her brows, Mildred said, "I don't, but I think she was the type of person to make enemies. Normally I never talk ill of people, but she did have some people who weren't too happy with her. Not that I know anything for certain, I just happened to overhear some conversations she had with people when she was talking on her cell phone."

"She had a cell phone here?"

Mildred nodded. "She never gave up all her *Englisch* ways when she came back to the community. I was sure I heard her talking in her room and I was certain she must've had a phone. I found the phone when I was cleaning her room. I was frightened to talk to her and have her yell at me again, but I knew I had to say something so I did. She spoke real nasty and told me never to tell anyone about it, and I didn't. I never even told Nehemiah about the cell phone. He wouldn't have liked her having something like that in the *haus*, and Camille knew that."

"*Nee, nee,* of course not." Ettie frowned and thought back to a couple of years ago when she and Elsa-May had kept a cell phone for emergencies. Until one day they had a visit from the bishop and he let them know he was aware of their phone. Elsa-May decided they should get rid of the phone after that. "And you heard her talking on her phone, arguing with someone?"

"Jah."

"Did you hear enough to know who it was, or what the argument was about?"

Mildred moved uncomfortably in her chair. "Some woman, I think it was. She was upset with Camille about something from the sounds of it. That's all I know."

"Interesting," Ettie said. "How did you know it was a woman she was speaking with?"

"The voice was loud enough for me to hear that it was a woman's voice."

Ettie sipped on her tea, knowing her next stop had to be Ronald Bradshaw, the neighbor who was so interested in the farm.

The rattle of a wagon, and loud sounds of horses' hooves, told the ladies that someone had pulled up outside the house.

"That will be Jacob come home for the midday meal."

"Is that the time already? I must be on my way."

"Stay! Ettie, you'll stay won't you?"

The back door swung open and Ettie leaned forward to see Jacob taking off his boots. He looked across into the kitchen. "Ettie."

"Hello, Jacob."

When he took his hat off and ran his large hand through his thick black hair, Ettie couldn't help comparing him to Nehemiah; the two were so similar in appearance.

"You're staying to have a meal with us, Ettie?" Jacob asked when he stepped into the kitchen.

Ettie looked back at Mildred who nodded, urging her to stay. *"Jah, denke.* I'll stay."

"After we eat, Jacob can run you home instead of you taking a taxi," Mildred said.

"I'm happy to do that, Ettie. I've got my wagon and horses just outside and you don't live that far away, do you?"

"Not far at all." Ettie smiled and thanked Jacob, but wasn't too happy that her visit to Ronald Bradshaw would have to be delayed until the next day. She could hardly ask Jacob to take her to the neighbor's farm and wait there while she talked to him. Besides, she couldn't let Mildred and Jacob know she intended to talk to their unfriendly neighbor.

While Ettie enjoyed Mildred's cooking, she felt a little bad for leaving Elsa-May on her own with her bad leg. She should've been there to help her get something to eat at least. Elsa-May would be able to make it to the kitchen, but it would be difficult.

CHAPTER 3

*W*hile Jacob drove her home in his wagon, Ettie knew she'd have to ask him some difficult questions if she was going to be any help to him. She bit the inside of her lip and tried to muster up some courage. "You know, Jacob, it doesn't look good for you that your *schweschder's* been murdered and the pair of you were known to fight all the time."

Jacob frowned at Ettie. "Arguing is one thing, Ettie, and murder is another. I couldn't kill anyone. I wouldn't have returned to the community if I didn't want to follow *Gott's* ways. I held no bad feelings against my *schweschder;* it was she who had bad feelings toward me. I let her know I didn't like the way she spoke to our *mudder.*"

Jacob always referred to his stepmother as his mother, never making the distinction that she wasn't his birth mother.

"*Jah,* I know that. I'm just saying how it looks for you. Sometimes when the police have no suspects their attention turns to the most likely person. Then, rather than innocent until proven guilty, it becomes a matter of having to prove that you are innocent."

Jacob looked over at Ettie and smiled. "Ettie, you're worrying too much about things. *Denke* for your concern; it's nice to know you care so much."

"I think you should be concerned."

"Why? The police questioned me and I told them everything I know. They seemed to be satisfied and I haven't done anything wrong."

Ettie sucked her lips in.

Jacob glanced at Ettie's concerned face, and then tipped his straw hat slightly back on his head. "You must tell me if you know something I don't. I know you've got contacts with the police since you've been involved with things like this before. I heard what happened to Horace, and *mamm's* told me about a few other things you've been involved in as well."

"I can tell you this: no matter what they've said to you, or wanted you to believe, it's clear that you're one of their suspects. I know that much. Well, most likely their only one so far, and that's why the detective has been out here trying to question people. No one will talk to him, apart from you it seems, and that's why he, the detective, asked me to help. Detective Kelly doesn't believe you did it, but I don't think he knows enough about Camille's life to know who could have done it or where to look for the person who killed her."

"The person who took her life might not have known her. It could've been a stranger, someone passing through."

"Possibly, but I believe she was the type of person to clash with people."

"Probably, because she was never happy at home. She never called Mildred *'mamm' or 'mudder;'* she always called her 'Mrs. Esh', if she had to call her something at all. Behind her back she would call her 'it' or 'the thing', but never if Mildred or *Dat* could hear her."

"I didn't realize things were that bad."

"They were. When *Mamm,* our real *mamm,* got sick, she beat Camille a couple of times. That's when *Dat* took our *mudder* to the doctor and found out about her mental illness."

Ettie gasped. "She was beaten? The poor little mite."

Jacob nodded. "Beaten and treated badly. I was older and out of the *haus* a lot with *Dat,* so that's why I escaped a lot of *Mamm's* nastiness."

"I had no idea things were like that."

"*Mamm* couldn't help it. It was the illness that made her act like that."

"All the same, it's awful for Camille to have gone through something like that."

"I think that's why she never took to Mildred. I don't think she could ever trust anyone."

"It's dreadful to think that one of the people who were supposed to love and protect her would do something like that."

"My *mudder* couldn't help it, Ettie. She was sick in the head," Jacob repeated. "I feel guilty that I didn't protect Camille."

"You shouldn't feel guilty. You were still so young yourself."

"Maybe that's why she hated me, because I wasn't there to look after her like a big *bruder* should've. Camille only got along with *Dat.*"

"That's dreadful."

Jacob nodded. "Anyway, I try not to think about the past. I try and remember my *mudder* how she used to be before she got sick."

Ettie nodded. "That's best."

"Now, no need to worry yourself about me, Ettie. Seems like I'm in the clear if the detective knows I didn't do it."

"He needs to investigate the thing properly. Do you know anyone who had the slightest possible reason to kill her? Did she have any arguments or disagreements with anyone that you know about?"

Jacob laughed. "She argued with *Mamm* every day of her life."

"I know they never got along."

"It was never *Mamm's* fault. She's always done everything she could to be a proper *mudder* to us."

"Did she have any disagreements with anyone apart from Mildred?"

"My *schweschder* and I were never close, as you know. I didn't know her well enough to know the enemies she made. I'm guessing there were a few."

"Do you know that for certain?"

"*Nee,* I'm just guessing, going by what type of person she was." Jacob glanced over at Ettie. "She wasn't a happy person, and the only time I saw her smile was whenever she was making someone miserable. The last days before she left the community, she had my *mudder* in tears every single day."

"That was after your *vadder* died?"

Jacob nodded. *"Jah,* she was much worse when she found out that the farm was left entirely to me."

"Mildred tells me you offered Camille half the farm?"

"She told you?"

Ettie nodded.

"Jah, I offered her half. It wasn't as though I talked *Dat* into leaving it all to me, but that's the idea Camille had gotten into her head. I didn't know who he was leaving it to; he never even talked of having a will. *Dat* left me a letter with his will telling me he was leaving it to me because he didn't want Camille interfering with the running of it, and he wanted Mildred to be able to stay on. I didn't exactly offer Camille half; I offered her forty nine percent so I could keep a controlling interest, and also that way *Mamm* wouldn't be turned out of the *haus."*

"I heard your *vadder* had money put away for Camille?"

Jacob glanced over at Ettie. "How did you know? *Ach,* I suppose *Mamm* told you that too. *Dat* had over two hundred and twenty-five thousand dollars for her."

Ettie gasped in shock and her hand flew to her mouth. "I never dreamed it would be so much."

"Dat's life savings. *Mamm* only wanted to live in the *haus;* she wasn't interested in money. She knew I'd take care of her."

"Who does the money go to now that...?"

"Camille left everything to me. I was a little pleased that she must've liked me deep down."

Ettie frowned. "That is a surprise, but I suppose her *vadder* dying gave her cause to think of writing her own will. She must have had a change of heart, then, where you were concerned. Perhaps it was your generous offer regarding the farm?"

"Nee." Jacob laughed and then moved the wagon over closer to the side of the road so a car could pass. When the car had zoomed past, Jacob said, "She didn't see my offer as generous at all. She wanted the whole lot and thought I was the one who was being unreasonable."

"Did she know why your *vadder* left the farm to you?"

"She never saw the letter *Dat* wrote to me if that's what you're asking. Camille knew *Dat* wasn't happy with the job she'd done of running the farm when she was in control of it."

"Surely she should've been happy with the money?"

Jacob shook his head. *"Nee,* she wasn't happy with anything, but that's the type of person she was."

"I suppose it does make sense that Camille left everything to you, after all, you were her only relative. And according to you and Mildred, she didn't make friends easily."

Jacob shrugged. "I guess she must've cared about me after all, in some way at least."

They were getting closer to Ettie's house and she had only a small amount of time left to talk to him. She needed to get as much information as she could. "So, can you think of anyone at all who might have wanted her gone?" She'd asked the question before but in a slightly different way. Ettie wasn't expecting a different answer to the one he'd already given her, but she was hoping.

He shook his head. "I've no idea."

Ettie pointed up the road. "It's the one up there on the left with the white fence."

When Jacob stopped his wagon right in front of Ettie's house, he jumped down to help her out.

"*Denke*. That's quite a distance for an old lady."

Jacob chuckled.

"Will you come in?" Ettie asked.

"*Nee*, I must get back home. I've got some men working for me today. I've got to get back to tell them what to do next. Say hello to Elsa-May for me."

"I will." Ettie stood at the gate and watched Jacob lead his two horses to turn the wagon around and head back down the road.

CHAPTER 4

*E*ttie started out bright and early the next morning to get to Ronald Bradshaw's house. She had the taxi drop her up the road so she would avoid being seen by Mildred and Jacob Esh.

When Ettie knocked on the door of the Bradshaw house, she waited and there was no answer. She knocked and waited again, but when there was still no answer she walked around to the back of the house.

"What are you doing?" a man's loud voice boomed, causing Ettie to jump.

Ettie's heart pounded, and she turned around to see the man she'd seen the day before when he was staring at Mildred's house. "Oh, forgive me. I was looking for a man named Bradshaw."

The man had a smudge of dirt across the left side of his face. Ettie tried not to look at the odd combination of frayed cut-off shorts and huge work boots he was wearing.

He took a couple of steps toward her. "That's me – Ron Bradshaw."

"Nice to meet you; I'm Ettie Smith. I've come to talk to you about Camille from next door."

"She died, didn't she?"

"I'm afraid so. I hope you don't mind if I ask you a few questions?"

The man frowned at her. "Depends what kinda questions you might be askin'."

"Did you ask Camille if she'd sell you the farm?"

"Ask?" he shook his head. "She came to me and said she'd sell it and asked me how much I'd pay. I've had my eye on that piece of land for years."

"Did Camille know that?"

"I wouldn't know, but I asked her father a couple times if he'd sell. He might have told her I wanted it, for all I know."

"I see. That's interesting."

"That woman and I agreed on a price and once the old man got sicker, she wanted more money."

"Really? But it wasn't hers to sell."

"She said the old man was dying and she'd get it when he kicked the bucket."

Ettie nodded and wondered whether Camille had used those exact words.

"Yeah. She was a nasty piece of work, that old woman." The man looked Ettie up and down. "You a friend of the family or somethin'?"

"I am." Ettie licked her lips. "Did you mean you were talking to Camille or her mother? Camille wasn't that old."

The man scratched his balding head. "Dunno. The one I was talking to was around forty or fifty. She said she was the daughter." He shook his head. "I'm no good with women's ages. Why do ya want to know?"

"Surely you know who's who if you've lived here for a long time. Camille grew up next door."

The man shook his head. "They keep to themselves. I've only noticed one woman there lately."

"Did you only talk to one woman from next door?"

The man nodded. "Are they thinking of sellin' now?"

"I don't think they are. They seem happy to keep it; it's been in the family for generations. The son inherited it from the father." Ettie breathed out heavily. She had to find out which woman he'd been talking with. Surely he wouldn't call Camille 'old'. What if he'd been speaking to Mildred thinking she was Camille? "Camille would have been around forty and her stepmother, Mrs. Esh, is in her late fifties."

"Can't help you." The man scratched his cheek. "I hear they think the woman – Camille – was murdered?"

Ettie nodded. "That's right."

He scratched his head. "That explains why she didn't get back to me." He stared at Ettie with his blue eyes piercing through her. "How did they do it?"

"Poison, I believe."

"Can't say I blame who did it. Shame she didn't sell me the farm first." He rubbed his gray stubbly chin.

"You didn't, or rather, you don't know the people next door very well at all, by the sounds."

His mouth turned down and he shook his head. "I talked to the old man maybe twice, I've spoken to the son about the same, and that woman a few times when she was offering to sell me the farm. That's it."

"You don't know Camille other than her talking to you about selling the farm? You've had no other dealings with her?"

"No, why should I?"

"Well, you lived in this house, on this farm, when Camille and her brother were growing up. You've been here for a long time, haven't you?"

"I've been here all me life. The missus and me raised the kids here. You should know that you folk keep to yourselves. I knew there were a couple of kids living there some years ago. When the woman came knocking on the door, I didn't even know who she was until she told me. After that, I saw her in town having an argument with some woman, and that was the only times I seen 'er."

"So only when she was talking about selling the farm to you, and the one time you saw her in town?"

"Yeah! That's right."

"She was arguing with someone, you say?"

"Yeah, a woman."

"Can you remember what the woman looked like?"

He shrugged his shoulders. "Never took much notice." He stared at Ettie and she noticed his eyes opened wider. "Do you think that woman might have been the one who done away with 'er?"

Ettie shrugged. "Do you remember how long ago it was?"

"Not long ago, not long ago at all. Couldn't say exactly when. I go into town on a Tuesday mostly, so yeah, it must've been a Tuesday."

"Thank you. You've been helpful."

"Why are ya askin'?" He repeated his earlier question:

"Do ya think the one she was arguing with did away with her?"

"I couldn't say." Ettie swallowed hard. The man had been polite enough, but Ettie had a feeling the man might have another side to him. He scared her a little. "I'm just a friend of the family, and I was a friend of Camille."

"Humph. I didn't think the woman would've had any friends. She was a liar and a cheat."

"Because she didn't get the farm in the will? I'm sure she would've kept her word to you if she had."

The old man chuckled. Was he happy that Camille didn't inherit the farm even though it meant he missed out on buying it?

"Is there anythin' else I can do ya for?" he asked, narrowing his eyes at Ettie.

"No. Thank you," Ettie said as she walked a few steps away, and then said, "Do you mind if I borrow your phone to call a taxi?"

"I'll call one for you," he said.

"Thank you. I'll wait down by the road."

The man nodded and Ettie headed to the road. Her first stop would be Detective Kelly to tell him what she'd learned so far.

CHAPTER 5

When the taxi pulled up at the police station, Ettie hoped the detective would be about. She climbed up the steps and walked inside. Before she could ask the officer behind the front desk if Detective Kelly was in, he walked up behind her.

"Mrs. Smith."

Ettie turned around to see Kelly with a takeout coffee in one hand and a white paper bag in the other.

"Detective, I've come to see you."

"Good. Come through to my office."

Ettie knew the way. His office used to be Detective Crowley's office before he had retired. When she sat in the chair opposite Kelly, she said, "I hope I'm not interrupting your lunch."

"Not at all. Not if you don't mind if I eat." He glanced at his watch. "I've got appointments the rest of the afternoon."

"Please, eat away. Don't mind me."

Detective Kelly smiled as he ripped open the white

paper bag to reveal two donuts. One had pink icing with sprinkles and the other was covered with a thick layer of chocolate.

"Detective, I hope this isn't your lunch?"

Kelly frowned and looked a little guilty as he stared at the donuts. "I have few pleasures in life, Mrs. Smith. Don't make me feel bad about one of the few things that makes me happy."

"I'm not saying don't eat things like that, but for lunch? That's not going to sustain a busy man like you with all the stress you must have."

Kelly pressed his lips together and flipped off the lid of his coffee. "And I suppose coffee's bad too?"

Ettie pulled a face. "Depends how many cups you have a day."

"Why have you come, Mrs. Smith? Have you found something out for me already?" he asked before he broke off a portion of his pink donut.

"I didn't pick you to be a cake-eater. When I asked you if you wanted tea or cake yesterday at my home, you turned it down." Crowley had never once turned down her or Elsa-May's cakes. "That's why I'm so surprised to see you eating something like this instead of a proper lunch."

Kelly finished his mouthful and said, "I don't know – I could've just eaten before I arrived, I can't recall. Does that bother you, that I didn't eat your cake?"

Ettie gave a little laugh at how ridiculous that sounded. "It's just that I formed an opinion of you and now I realize I was wrong."

The detective nodded. "I've learned never to form an opinion of anyone too early. Also, even if you know someone well, they can always do something that surprises even themselves."

"I suppose that's a good lesson to learn."

Kelly's glance at his watch prompted Ettie to get to the point of why she was there. "I went out to visit Camille's mother yesterday, and then today I talked to the neighbor, Ronald Bradshaw. It seems that the neighbor wanted the land. Camille had agreed to sell it to him when she thought she'd be getting the land when her father died."

"How did the old man die?"

Ettie frowned. "He's not dead. I just talked to him this morning."

"No, not that one – Nehemiah Esh."

"Oh." Ettie's gaze flickered to the ceiling. "Old age, I'd say. Wait a minute, he might have had a problem with his heart or something along those lines."

"Hmm." Kelly popped the last of the pink donut in his mouth. Ettie couldn't help frowning at him in disgust. "Was there an autopsy?" he asked.

"No, nothing like that. I don't think so. Come to think of it, I don't know the answer to that. Why? Do you think he might have been killed as well?"

"No." The detective shook his head then looked across at Ettie. "Why? Do you?"

"I've never given any thought to it."

"It's interesting when you talk about the will, and people waiting to pounce on the farm right after the old man dies."

Ettie said, "I don't think it was like that. There was no one waiting to pounce. According to the neighbor he'd asked them before if they wanted to sell. I don't think anyone was waiting for Nehemiah to die. The neighbor said he talked to Camille, Nehemiah, and Jacob separately about wanting to buy the farm."

"Was it a sudden death?" Kelly picked up the chocolate donut and took a huge bite.

"Nehemiah's?"

The detective nodded and Ettie pretended not to look at the chocolate sprinkles that clung to the sides of the detective's mouth. "I believe he was sick for quite some time. He went downhill rapidly and was in quite a bit of pain. Come to think of it, I think Mildred mentioned it was his heart."

After Kelly swallowed, he said, "I didn't think that was painful."

Ettie shrugged. "I'm certain it is."

Kelly licked his lips, and then wiped his mouth with a paper napkin. "What else did you find out?"

"I talked to Jacob and found out that after Camille discovered he'd been left the farm, she was terribly upset. Jacob even ended up offering her forty nine percent of the farm."

The detective nodded before he took a mouthful of coffee. "Yes, that's what he tried to tell us."

Ettie raised her eyebrows. "Tried to tell you? You mean you don't believe him?"

"There's no proof, is there? It seems a generous offer for someone to make."

"Anyway, she turned it down," Ettie said. "She wanted the entire farm – one hundred percent."

"We've only his word on that," Detective Kelly said. "Do you know about the money she inherited?"

Ettie said, "To be accurate, I don't think that she inherited it. It was banked for her well before Nehemiah died."

"Are you talking about the trust fund?"

"Yes," Ettie said.

"Jacob told us about the trust fund and you're right, it wasn't an inheritance. It was a trust fund that her father set up for her. The thing was that Jacob had control of it. Nehemiah Esh wasn't a smart man."

"Detective!"

Kelly took a mouthful of coffee and then brought the cup down to the desk. "You've got two siblings that don't get along; you don't put one in charge of the other's money. Not a smart move."

"He most likely had his reasons."

"Only if he wanted them to hate each other more."

Ettie wasn't pleased that the detective knew that Jacob and Camille didn't get along. That wouldn't be good for Jacob.

"I'll make a note to look into that fund and see how much of it's left." The detective had another mouthful of coffee. "I'm sorry, do you want tea or coffee? I'll have someone make you one if you do. It mightn't be very good – that's why I get mine from the coffee shop down the road."

"No. I'm fine, thank you." Did Kelly think Jacob might have spent some of Camille's money?

The detective rubbed his hands together, picked up a pen and wrote something down on his notepad. When he finished, he looked up. "Did you find anything else out?"

"Yes, it seems that Camille had quite a few people she didn't get along with. She was seen in town arguing with a woman, and Mildred heard her speaking on a cell phone arguing with a woman as well."

The detective screwed up the white paper takeout bag and tossed it in the trash basket. Once he had his pen in hand again, he asked, "Do you have any names?"

"No, I don't, but that's good, isn't it? She had other people she didn't get along with."

"Good for Jacob?"

"Yes."

The detective stared at Ettie before he took another mouthful of coffee. "We'll see." He rose to his feet with his coffee in hand. "Thank you, Mrs. Smith. You've been a great help. I'd still like you to keep your eyes and ears open. I might still need your help depending on how things go."

"I'd be glad to help anytime." Ettie stood up, said goodbye, and walked out the door. She suddenly turned and walked back into Kelly's office.

Kelly was now sitting down at his desk. He looked up at her. "Yes, Mrs. Smith?"

She studied his face. Could he be keeping something from her? "Nothing, Detective." Ettie walked away feeling she was getting far too suspicious of people.

CHAPTER 6

*E*ttie was pleased to get home and she told Elsa-May every detail of the conversations she'd had and all she'd found out that day. "Well, what do you make of it all?"

Elsa-May was knitting as usual and had her sore leg elevated on a chair. "The man next door doesn't seem sure who he was speaking with. Was he speaking with Camille or was he speaking to Mildred?"

"That's what I wondered at first, but Mildred said she had no interest in the farm and only wanted to stay on there. She didn't feel the need to own the farm or have any part of the ownership. I don't think she'd be running over to the man next door to do a deal behind everyone's backs. She didn't want to be left anything. She didn't even want any money. *Nee!* The neighbor must have been speaking to Camille because she had expected that she'd inherit the farm."

"Strange."

"Do you think that's strange?"

Elsa-May nodded. "A little strange that she didn't want to own the house or anything when she's got a step-daughter like Camille who'd be pleased to see her off the property. She was taking a risk relying solely on Jacob."

"I disagree. Jacob will always look after his *mudder*. Jacob and Mildred are like real *mudder* and son."

"Even so, she seems a little naive."

"How so?"

Elsa-May rubbed her leg. "From what you told me, the detective might think that someone killed Nehemiah since he was questioning you about his death."

Ettie regretted telling Elsa-May so many details. *"Jah,* I think he might."

"And it sounds like Camille had many enemies."

"I'm hoping that Jacob's in the clear. Kelly said he believes he's innocent."

Elsa-May added, "I hope that's right."

"Well, I'd better go and fix the dinner. Speaking about food, you should have seen what Kelly ate for lunch. I was so surprised and you would've had something to say about it if you'd been there too." Ettie told Elsa-May about the detective's eating habits and Elsa-May had a good chuckle. "It's dreadful, Elsa-May. It's not a laughing matter. He can't go on eating like that every day."

"Hmm. Why don't you cook up some extra dinner tonight, and then take him some food tomorrow? I'm sure he'd appreciate a decent meal rather than having sweets."

"That's a good idea. I'll do that."

~

THE NEXT DAY, Ettie had fixed some sausage and egg casserole to take to detective Kelly, and since he had a sweet tooth, she'd gone to the trouble of making him some blueberry muffins. She placed the bowls in a cloth bag and walked down the road to call for a taxi. As soon as the taxi stopped, a small man in long cream-colored pants and a matching short-sleeved shirt sprang out and opened the front passenger-side door for her.

"Such service! Thank you."

"No problem at all, lady."

He seemed such a happy man that Ettie was certain she was in for a pleasant drive, but as soon as she sat in the seat, heavy cigarette smoke invaded her nostrils. She wound down the window and inhaled some fresh air before the driver got in the car. Normally Ettie didn't mind a little smoke, but the odor in the taxi was overpowering. She glanced down at an overflowing ashtray between the two seats and crinkled her nose. She was glad the muffins in her lap were covered in heavy cloths and the casserole was in a tightly-lidded glass bowl so they wouldn't pick up the smoky smell.

"Where to?" the driver asked while he fastened his seat belt.

Ettie was tempted to make a comment about him fastening his seat belt but not being concerned how many cigarettes he was smoking. She held her tongue.

"Where to?" he asked again glancing over at her.

"The police station."

He flicked the meter on while he pulled away from the shoulder. When he turned onto the main road, he lit up a cigarette. He drew in a long breath, and then blew it out the partially opened window. Ettie glanced in his direction to see smoke wafting out of his nose in waves. Then she looked directly ahead hoping the fabric in her clothes and her prayer *kapp* wouldn't pick up the smell.

Suddenly the taxi driver asked, "Are you a relative of the Amish man who was arrested last night?"

"What man?"

"I heard it on the radio. Some Amish man was just arrested for murdering his sister."

Ettie's mouth fell open. It could only be Jacob who had been arrested. There had been no other murder in the Amish community. "Put your foot on it, driver!" Ettie yelled.

The man did as instructed.

"I'm not a relative. I'm a good friend and I believe I've been double-crossed."

The taxi driver gave her a sideways look and remained silent the rest of the trip. When the taxi pulled up, Ettie threw down some money hoping it was enough to cover the fare. The driver got out of the car to help Ettie out, but by the time he reached the passenger side of the car she was halfway up the steps of the station.

Once she was through the door, she hurried to the man sitting behind the front desk. "Where's Detective Kelly?"

The man looked up at her with a bored face, and drawled, "He's busy at the moment, ma'am."

"I need to see him immediately. Let him know Ettie Smith is here, would you? Now?"

"What's it regarding?"

"He'll know."

"Take a seat and I'll call him." The officer picked up his phone and talked to Kelly, and when he placed the receiver down, he called out to Ettie, "He'll be out as soon as he can."

"How long will that be?"

He shook his head. "I'm not sure."

Ettie stood up with the bundle of food still in her arms, and walked over to the officer. "Then I'd like to speak to Jacob Esh."

"Who?"

"I believe you have him here somewhere. He's just been arrested."

"No, you can't talk to anyone in custody. Please take a seat and Detective Kelly will be out to see you as soon as he can."

Ettie narrowed her eyes at the officer, and then turned and took a seat. It was an hour later when Detective Kelly finally came out to see her.

"Come through," he said, motioning to her with his hand.

Ettie followed him through to his office with the bag of food clutched in her hands. Once he was seated, she placed the food on his desk without any explanation of what it was, sat down, and then asked, "What's going on, Detective? You've arrested Jacob?"

He interlocked his fingers, placing them under his chin. "We have him in for questioning. He's not under arrest, not at all."

"The taxi driver said he heard on the radio that an Amish man was under arrest for killing his sister."

"I said he's not under arrest. I'd hardly think a taxi

driver is a reliable source of information." The detective sniffed the air. "Do you smoke?"

"No, I do not." Just as she'd feared, her clothes had picked up the odor in the taxi.

"I can smell cigarette smoke. I'm sensitive to the smell. I've given them up."

"Congratulations," Ettie said sarcastically before she regretted her tone. She licked her lips, about to make an apology and explain about the smoke-filled taxi she'd ridden in to get there, when the detective spoke.

"I'm afraid there was more to things than I let on to you."

Ettie tipped her head to one side. "What haven't you told me?"

"The kind of things that made it look like Jacob Esh murdered his sister."

Ettie pulled her mouth to one side. "I didn't know there were things that made him look guilty. You said…"

"There are."

"Can you be more specific?"

The detective leaned back in his chair and scratched his forehead. "We had dealings with Camille before she died. She'd had shots fired into her apartment. Someone drove past and shot into her home three times. More accurately, it was a drive-by shooting and three shots were fired."

Ettie gasped.

The detective nodded. "Someone tried to kill her."

"You think it was Jacob?"

"Evidence strongly points to him. He'd hardly be

sticking to your Amish rules if he was about to kill some-one. He could've paid someone to shoot her, or he could've borrowed a car and done the job himself. I know you were just about to point out to me that he doesn't own a car."

"Were the gunshots to scare her or kill her?"

"I don't know what you're getting at, Mrs. Smith, but when someone has a gun fired into their home, we take it that the person or persons involved who were doing the shooting were aiming to kill."

"Was it while she was living in her apartment? Because Mildred never mentioned anything about a gun being fired into her home."

"It was after she left the house and started living in the apartment."

"So after her father's death, then? Because that's when she left the house, when she found out she hadn't been left the farm."

"Yes, that's right."

"There's no motive for him to kill her. He already had the farm."

"There's the money. People have killed for a lot less."

"So, you've got Jacob here still?"

"He's still being questioned. I've already grilled him but he's sticking to the same story so I'm letting someone else have a crack at him."

"Have you considered that he might be telling the truth?"

"Someone's dead, Mrs. Smith. If the brother didn't do it, then who did?"

"In just one day I found out that Camille had enemies;

two people told me that. Why don't you look into those people?"

Kelly sighed. "I thank you for your help, but I think you've done all you can do. I hoped you'd uncover something we didn't know, but it seems there is nothing we didn't already know."

"You think he's guilty, and you thought he was guilty all along, which means you tricked me into believing you were trying to help him."

"I had to make you think I was on his side. I knew you wouldn't help if you thought otherwise."

Ettie rose to her feet. She bit her tongue while thinking of all the things she wanted to say to the despicable person before her. "I can't speak the words on my mind right now." She pushed the food she'd brought toward him. "Elsa-May thought you should have some proper food at lunchtime." Ettie turned and walked out the door without saying goodbye.

She heard him call after her: "Wait, Mrs. Smith."

Ettie turned around.

"I couldn't tell you. It would have influenced your thinking when you were finding things out for me."

Ettie folded her arms firmly in front of her chest. "That's something Crowley never would've done. He was always honest with us and we respected him for it."

"Mrs. Smith, I do appreciate your help, but I'll handle things from here."

"You told me you thought he was innocent. That's the only reason I helped you."

"Like I said, I had to tell you something to get you on my side."

Ettie opened her mouth in shock. "That's unethical and downright disgusting."

Kelly smirked. "I didn't want to deceive you; it's just part of the job sometimes. Often it's the only way we can get things done."

"So you do think Jacob's guilty for certain?"

"Have you come up with any other suspects?"

"I told you; there's the neighbor, and the woman Camille was seen arguing with in town. Maybe there were two people she was arguing with, because Mildred heard her arguing with someone on her phone and the neighbor saw her arguing with a woman in town."

"Hearsay and conjecture. It's too fuzzy a lead to follow up. I need something concrete."

"Everything is fuzzy until you follow the leads and see where they take you."

"Are you telling me how to do my job?"

"Yes, I suppose I am. Because if you think that Jacob is guilty, you're not doing a good job right now."

"You think he's innocent because he's a part of your community?"

Ettie shook her head. "It's not that."

"I think we're through speaking for today."

"What? Until the next time you need my help?"

The detective frowned and threw his hands in the air. "It doesn't please me that I had to lie to you, but that's just what had to happen."

Ettie pressed her lips together. "You don't mind if I follow some leads that you're ignoring, do you?"

"As long as you don't get in my way you are at liberty to do as you wish."

The detective reached out and grabbed a piece of paper from his desk. He motioned for her to come forward and she did so. "I'll tell you what. Since you're so upset with me, I'll give you a peace offering." He tossed the sheet of paper to Ettie. "This is a list of names and addresses of the people Camille talked to most often from her cell phone."

Ettie took hold of the paper and stared at it. There weren't many names on it. She looked up at the detective. "Isn't this against some kind of law, letting me have this list?"

The detective smiled. He swiveled in his chair and turned his head away. "I can't help it if the list disappeared from my office. If I need the list, I'll just print out another one. Maybe I never printed one out at all."

Ettie looked down at the paper, holding it tightly, and then disappeared out of his office without saying goodbye. He didn't deserve a goodbye. Ettie was mad with herself for not figuring out what Kelly had been up to from the start. She wasn't normally fooled so easily, and now she was so upset she was nauseous.

CHAPTER 7

*a*fter Ettie left the station, she hailed a taxi, knowing she had to go and see her dear friend, Mildred.

When the taxi pulled up at Mildred's house, she could see the bishop's buggy leaving. Well, at least she had someone to speak with this morning. When Ettie's taxi drove off, a teary-eyed Mildred met her at the front door. "I'm so glad you've come. You've heard what's happened?"

"I have." Ettie put her arm around Mildred as she broke down and sobbed. "Come on, let's sit inside."

Once they were sitting down in the living room, Mildred sniffed back her tears. "They came here with so many police cars; lights were whirling and flashing, and then they stormed in here and said they had a search warrant. Then they went right through the house, and the barn, and took things away with them."

"What kind of things?" Ettie was amazed that Kelly

had never mentioned the search warrant or the fact that the police had taken things.

"I didn't see exactly what they took from the barn, but they took all Jacob's hunting guns that he had kept in the house for safety. They think that Jacob killed Camille, but she wasn't shot. Why would they take the guns?"

"She had gunshots fired into her apartment. She didn't tell you?"

Mildred opened her mouth wide. When Ettie saw the hurt in Mildred's eyes she regretted asking the question. Ettie knew how painful it was for Mildred that Camille resented her. Of course Camille wouldn't have told her about the attempt on her life.

"I don't know how to help him, Ettie. I found a card from a lawyer amongst Nehemiah's things." Mildred stood up and walked over to a small bureau, found a business card, and brought it back to Ettie.

Ettie took the card and read the name. "Claymore Cartwright." Ettie looked at the back of the well-worn card and read the address. "He's just in town, if he's still in business. I'll go with you if you want to see him."

"Would you, Ettie?"

"*Jah*. Do you want me to call now and make an appointment?"

Mildred nodded.

Ettie rose to her feet with the card in hand. "I'll do it right away. You stay here and take some deep breaths. Do you want a cup of tea?"

"*Nee*, I had tea just now with the bishop."

"*Jah*, I just passed him when I came through your gate."

Ettie made her way to the barn. She pushed the door open and saw things scattered everywhere. The police must've done this. No one would keep their barn in a state like this. She stepped over things and made her way to the telephone on the other side of the barn. She picked up the receiver and dialed the number on the card. Ettie was pleased when she heard it ring – that meant the man was still in business.

After a couple of weird dial-tone and clicking sounds on the other end of the phone, a male voice answered. It was the lawyer himself. Once Ettie explained the situation to the lawyer, he had them come in immediately. Ettie called for a taxi, placed the receiver back on the hook, and hurried to tell Mildred.

ETTIE CONVINCED Mildred to take the taxi in to visit with the lawyer rather than taking the buggy, figuring they should get there as fast as possible.

When they arrived in town, the taxi dropped them right outside the address that was on the old business card.

They took the elevator up to the fourth floor. When the elevator doors opened, they stepped out and followed the corridor around the corner. They were looking for the office of Claymore Cartwright, but it was nowhere to be seen. All the offices appeared to be empty. When they walked up to the end of the corridor, Ettie was pleased to see an open door. Ettie walked two more steps and when she peeped in she saw a young man behind a desk in a sparsely furnished office. The man was dressed in casual clothes and wore a bright green baseball cap.

He smiled and rose to his feet. "Mrs. Esh?"

Ettie was surprised that the man was so young. He had to be the lawyer, as he'd known Mildred's name. Given his name and the aged business card she had expected a much older man. Ettie nodded and pulled Mildred forward. "This is Mrs. Esh. I'm her friend, the one who called you. Ettie Smith."

"Please, come in."

Ettie had never seen a lawyer in casual clothes. She'd only seen them wear dark suits and ties.

"I heard that your son was arrested. Are you here because you want me to represent him?"

Ettie spoke first. "He's not been arrested, although the news stations seem to think so."

"Yes, they do like news - bad news, anyway - about the Amish."

"Seems so." Ettie continued, "He was taken in for questioning, and the police had a search warrant and took a great number of things out of Mildred's home and out of her barn."

Ettie glanced at Mildred, hoping she didn't mind her speaking on her behalf. Mildred wasn't used to doing things for herself because Nehemiah, or Jacob, had always been around to do things for her. Ettie looked back at the lawyer and continued, "Mildred found your card amongst her late husband's things, and we really need some legal advice. We're not too sure how these things work."

Claymore looked at Mildred. "I set a few things up for your husband."

"The bank trust fund?" Ettie asked.

"Yes," the lawyer said with a sharp nod. "I also helped him write his will."

Mildred finally spoke. "They took Jacob in the early hours this morning and searched all through our house and also our barn. The police took things away with them."

The lawyer leaned forward in his chair. "What did they take?"

"They took so many things. They asked about firearms, so I told them where Jacob kept his hunting rifles and they took all of them. Some were his father's, and some didn't even work. They also took things from the barn; I'm not sure what."

Ettie spoke again, "Before all this happened, the detective, Keith Kelly, asked for my help because no one in our Amish community would talk to him. He told me he thought that Jacob was innocent. I was only to find out later that he thought nothing of the kind."

The lawyer looked at Mildred. "Where's your son now?"

"He's at the police station."

"He shouldn't be questioned without a lawyer. I'll go and see what I can do."

"Could you do that?" Mildred asked.

"Yes, I'll see what I can find out."

"Have you done this kind of thing before?" Mildred asked.

Ettie knew Mildred was asking because he didn't look like a lawyer and his office didn't look like any lawyer's office she'd ever been to.

Claymore smiled as though he'd often answered that question. "Yes, I have. I do a bit of everything."

While the lawyer asked Mildred some background questions, Ettie took in her surroundings. There were only two small offices and no receptionist. He appeared to work by himself. There was no one in the other office, and from what she could see when she'd walked past it, it was bare. Ettie turned her head to view the small reception area through the open door of the office. There were a few filing cabinets and some ten large white folders on a book-shelf. Nothing about the office was plush or expensive.

As the lawyer stood up, he said, "Don't you ladies worry about anything. I'll go and see him right now and I'll give you a phone call this afternoon to let you know what's happening."

"Thank you, Mr. Cartwright," Mildred said. "Oh, and there's the matter of your fee."

The young lawyer waved his hand in the air. "Let's talk about that later. Don't concern yourself with that now. I can sort something out with your son."

The lawyer smiled at them as Ettie stood up and helped Mildred to her feet. Mildred looked as though she would cry again. Ettie wanted to get out of the office so Mr. Cartwright could lock up and go to see how he could help Jacob.

ALL ETTIE COULD DO WAS TAKE Mildred home and wait for a call from the lawyer. They'd opened the barn door so they could more easily hear the telephone while they sat in the room closest, which was the kitchen.

"*Ach*, Ettie. I've already lost Nehemiah and Camille was always lost; I can't lose Jacob as well. What if they've arrested him?"

"The detective didn't say he'd arrested him. In fact, he said he hadn't arrested him. I'm sure Jacob will be home as soon as they finish questioning him. At least he's got a lawyer with him now."

Mildred nodded. "I suppose I should've called a lawyer first thing when they took him." Tears trickled down Mildred's cheeks. "I don't know what I ever did to make Camille hate me so much."

Ettie leaned over and rubbed Mildred's arm. "I don't think she hated you. She was probably so upset over her *mudder's* death that she never got over it."

Mildred shook her head. "I don't know. She used to look at me with such hatred in her eyes." Mildred looked across at Ettie. "I've never seen anything like it. She used to scare me. I thought one time she was going to hit me."

"I didn't know things were that bad."

"I couldn't tell anyone how mean she was to me. Whenever she'd walk past me she'd push me or bump me. I didn't know whether it was my fault, if I'd done something to upset her, but Jacob was never like that toward me and I always treated him in the same way that I treated her. I gave them both the same discipline when they needed it and I tried to give them all the love that Mary would've."

The sound of a car humming up toward the house met

Ettie's ears. Mildred sprang to her feet and peered out the window.

"It's him. I think it's the lawyer. I can see two people in the car."

Ettie joined her at the window, and then Mildred sprinted to the front door. Ettie managed to catch up to her as Jacob got out of the lawyer's car. He straightened himself up. He looked dreadful. His face was white and he had deep circles under his eyes.

Mildred ran to him. "Are you all right?

"I am now that I'm home."

Mildred hugged Jacob and he put his arm around her shoulder. "It's okay, *Mamm.* Everything's gonna be okay. But right now I just wanna get some sleep."

"What happened? Didn't they feed you? Oh, you were there for so long. You looked dreadful."

Jacob shook his head. "I can't talk about anything right now. I just need to sleep." He nodded hello to Ettie, and then said, "Excuse me, will you?"

"Certainly," Ettie said.

Jacob turned around and shook the lawyer's hand.

"I'll be in touch." The lawyer slapped Jacob lightly on his back before Jacob walked into the house.

"Thank you for getting him out," Mildred said to the lawyer.

"We're not out of the woods yet. They didn't have anything to hold him on, but they seem pretty confident that they're getting some evidence soon. They're running ballistics tests on the bullets they found. And they mentioned they found fingerprints in Camille's apartment that didn't belong to her. They've taken his prints."

"So they didn't arrest him?" Mildred asked.

"They questioned him, or rather, grilled him. You should've called me sooner. He could've refused to answer."

"He's got nothing to hide." Mildred started blubbering again, so Ettie did her best to comfort her.

"He's home now," Ettie said. "Safe and sound."

"I've made a time with Jacob to come here tomorrow and go over a few things. All the guns they took from here have Jacob's prints on them."

A lawyer who makes house calls? Ettie then noticed that he was wearing different clothes than when he saw them in his office earlier that day. "You changed your clothes from this morning?"

"It was my day off. Your call was diverted to my mobile. I thought it sounded serious enough to forgo my free time."

Ettie smiled. "Thank you."

"Oh, we didn't know. That was so good of you."

He chuckled. "I changed my clothes before I went to the station. I always keep a suit in my office."

The lawyer said goodbye and the two ladies watched as his car hummed down the driveway.

"Such a nice young man, and handsome too," Ettie said.

"*Jah,* if only I was young again," Mildred added.

Ettie and Mildred looked at each other and giggled. "Well, at least we can find something to laugh about," Ettie said.

"You do cheer me up, Ettie. Will you stay for dinner?"

"*Nee denke.* Normally I would, but I'll have to get home

to see Elsa-May and fix her dinner. She's got a bad leg and can't walk very well."

"What's wrong with her leg?"

"I'm not certain. It started giving her some trouble a few days ago. If she keeps it elevated she says it doesn't hurt as much."

"Has she been to the doctor about it?"

"*Nee.*" Ettie pulled a face. "Why? Do you think she should?"

"I have heard that blood clots can give people sore legs. They can be very dangerous, and sometimes people even have to have their legs amputated."

Ettie gasped. It hadn't occurred to her that her sister could be in danger of something like that. "Well, it's too late to take her to the doctor now. I'll take her first thing in the morning."

On Ettie's way home, she stopped by Ava's place to see if her young friend could help with the list of names and addresses that Kelly had given her.

"I'M HERE to ask you to help me with something. You helped me before with Horace, so I was hoping you'd be able to help me again." Ettie filled Ava in with what she knew so far about Camille's murder and her life.

"I'll help in any way I can. What do you want me to do?"

Ettie pulled out the list of names that Kelly had allowed her to take. "I'm going to work through these one by one and see what I can find out. These are the people who Camille was speaking to from her cell phone. These are the names of the people she called, and those who called her."

"What do you want me to do? Come with you when you speak to them?"

Ettie passed the list to Ava and then said, "Firstly, I'd like you to see what you can find out about each one. I've been told she was having arguments with people, so…"

"How could I do that? You mean on the Internet?" Ava looked at the list.

"*Jah,* that, and have you still got that helpful friend who works at the DMV?"

Ava glanced up at Ettie. *"Jah,* I do."

"I'm hoping your friend can get us photos that match these phone numbers. And also verify that the addresses are current."

"I'll see what I can find out. I'm certain he'll help."

Ettie nodded. "Very good. Before I go home, I'll have a quick look through the *haus* to see what repairs need doing."

"Do you want me to come with you?"

"Nee, you look like you're busy cooking."

"I'll talk to my friend tonight, if I can, or first thing in the morning. I'm guessing you want the information quickly?"

Ettie smiled. "You know me well." After Ettie left Ava, she walked around to the front door of the main house. She bent down to fetch the key from under the potted fern at the front door. Once she pushed the rusty key into the lock, she turned it to the right and heard a loud click.

Ettie pushed the door open and a waft of stale, warm

air swept over her. "I must air the place out," she mumbled to herself. When Ettie walked further in, she realized how much she missed her dear friend, Agatha. They used to sit for hours and talk. Ettie wiped a tear from her eye and was a little sad that she'd never be able to live in this house. Not after they found poor old Horace dead under the floor.

The rocking chair was back in the middle of the floor where Ettie had left it last time she was in the house. The chair had always been placed right over poor old Horace. "I'll see you again when *Gott* takes me home, Agatha," Ettie muttered. Ettie blinked hard and reminded herself why she was there. There was no time to reflect on sentimental nonsense, not when Elsa-May was waiting for her to cook the dinner.

Ettie walked through the house, making a mental note of all the repairs she'd have to get Jeremiah to do. There were kitchen doors coming off their hinges, the ceiling had peeling paint, and some of the windows didn't open. There was mold in one corner of the living room, and she had noticed when she'd been unlocking the door that the boards on the porch needed replacing.

Ettie sighed. "So many things to do." Thankfully Agatha had also left her money. She could use that to fix the house, and then she'd lease it to a nice Amish family.

CHAPTER 8

*O*ver dinner with Elsa-May, Ettie brought up the subject of visiting a doctor.

"*Nee,* definitely not! I've had problems like this before and it just goes away."

"But what if it's something more serious this time?"

"Like what?" Elsa-May's eyebrows drew together.

"Mildred said it could be a blood clot."

Elsa-May's eyes opened wide. "Really? She's had experience with that kind of thing?"

"She's heard of it."

"Perhaps I should go."

"I think that's for the best. You haven't been yourself lately."

"I have been tired."

"And vague," Ettie added.

"Have I been vague?"

Ettie nodded. "And that's not like you."

"I have been concerned about Mildred being all on her own if something happens to Jacob."

"She'll be okay," Ettie said.

"She's quite frail, you know. I don't mean physically. She's relied on her husband all the time for everything, and now that he's gone I guess she's relying on Jacob. What will happen if...?"

"We can't think about that," Ettie said. "We'll have to keep our thoughts off the bad things."

"*Jah,* Ettie, you're right. And anyway, there are so many people in the community to help her and there's all the ladies in the knitting circle."

"I forgot she was in your knitting circle. And there's something else I forgot to tell you about."

"What is it, Ettie?"

"The detective gave me a list of names of the people who Camille called from her cell phone. And the people who called her."

"He just gave it to you?"

Ettie nodded. "Well, he didn't really give it to me. He told me he couldn't help the fact if someone took the list from his desk."

"Then he is on Jacob's side."

"I wouldn't say that. I was angry that he'd told me he believed Jacob and then I'd found out that he'd been stringing me along. It was more a peace-offering; *jah,* that's what he called it."

Elsa-May scratched the side of her forehead. "Don't you think that's a little dangerous if the woman was murdered? One of the people on the list could very well have killed her. Why would you put yourself in danger like that?"

Ettie shrugged. "Too late now. I was happy to stay out

of the whole thing. Detective Kelly was the one who knocked on our door. Jacob and Mildred need our help. I just can't turn my back on them."

"Let's just eat our food in silence," Elsa-May said in an angry tone.

Suits me just fine, Ettie thought.

THE NEXT DAY, Elsa-May and Ettie sat in the doctor's waiting room. The receptionist had fitted them into an eleven thirty appointment slot. Ettie tried to stop thinking about Jacob, and the information Ava might be able to find out, and did her best to concentrate on her sister.

When the doctor was ready, the receptionist told Elsa-May she could go in. Ettie stood up at the same time.

Elsa-May frowned at her. "You don't need to come in with me."

"I will. I want to hear what he says."

"Please yourself, then, but I think I have to give permission for you to go in with me." Elsa-May had a word to the nurse, and then both sisters went into the examination room.

When the doctor had finished examining Elsa-May, he gave them his conclusions. "You were right to come in. It could very well be a blood clot. I'll book you straight into the hospital for tests. You'll need to have a scan and the sooner the better."

Ettie was grateful for Mildred warning her of such a thing.

"I thought people only got clots if they were still for long stretches."

Ettie kept quiet, stopping herself from pointing out to Elsa-May that she sat down without moving for hours almost every day while she knitted.

"As people get older, they're more at risk, and with your weight problem it puts you in a high-risk category."

"I don't have a weight problem. I've always been on the bigger side."

The doctor stared at her and blinked a couple times. "You could do with losing some weight. Try taking a walk every morning and cut down on your food." The doctor looked across at his computer, and then said, "I'll call an ambulance to take you in."

"That's not necessary, surely!" Elsa-May barked.

"I'd prefer that we take precautions."

Ettie leaned over close to her, and said, "Do as he says, Elsa-May."

Elsa-May looked at the doctor. "Okay, have it your way."

The doctor smiled, and then turned back to his computer and tapped on a few keys. "I'm letting the hospital know you're coming, and arranging for an ambulance."

Once they were back in the waiting room of the clinic, Elsa-May turned to Ettie who was sitting next to her. "There's no point in you coming with me. Why don't you go and see what Ava has found out?"

"*Nee*, I'll wait with you."

"Just go, Ettie. Stop being so *schtarrkeppich*."

Elsa-May's comment made Ettie smile. It was she who

was the stubborn one. "All right, then. I'll come and check on you at the hospital after I've seen Ava."

"I'll get a taxi home when they've done the test."

"I should be at the hospital before you go. You might have a long wait before they can run the test. They've probably got a long line of people in front of you."

"Just go, Ettie, and stop being a mother hen. Jacob needs your help. I'm big enough to look after myself – too big, the doctor tells me." Elsa-May chuckled. "The doctor just doesn't realize I've got large bones."

"Okay, as long as you don't mind me going."

"Go!"

CHAPTER 9

*E*ttie went straight to Ava's place after she left Elsa-May to wait for the ambulance.

Ava had seen her arrive and she waited at the door of her *grossdaddi haus.* "I'm glad you've come when you did. I was just about to get ready, then I was going to drive over to your *haus* to see you."

"I wouldn't have been there. I've just taken Elsa-May to the doctor, and now she's waiting to be taken to the hospital for tests."

"Nothing serious, I hope."

"The doctor thinks she might have a blood clot so she needs to have a scan."

"I hope she'll be all right."

Ettie nodded. "She's in good hands."

"Come in, and I'll tell you what I've found out."

Once they were sitting at the small kitchen table, Ava said, "I noticed something on the list you gave me; the number of conversations the people had with Camille were written on the side." Ava picked up the list and pointed out the numbers to Ettie. "Now, you can see that most of the conversations on her cell were with a woman called Judith Mackelvanner."

"Did you find out about this woman?"

Ava passed over all the printouts from her friend at the DMV, including photos of all the people on Camille's phone list.

Ava pulled out the photo of the woman and tapped on it. "That's her there; she's a doctor. I 'Googled' her and found out that she works at the hospital, and she studies neurology. I know that because she's been looking for volunteers on some trials she's running for a paper she's writing."

"Was Camille one of her volunteers?"

Ava shrugged her shoulders. "I don't know."

"Who else is on the list?"

"There was a call to a woman. Now this is interesting – her mobile phone records are in the name of Lacey Miller, but the DMV has that number down as belonging to a Leah Miller."

"Your friend traced the mobile numbers?"

"*Jah.* Now look at this photo of Leah Miller."

"That's Leah Miller who used to be in our community! She'd have to be right around the same age as Camille. That would be one of the *Englisch* friends she had that Mildred was speaking about."

"Yep. I remember her, and she certainly looks like the Leah we know."

"Camille had also called some businesses, and a few car places. It looks as though she might have been about to buy a car. There was also a call to someone called Nick Heaton."

"Who's he?"

"I looked him up on the computer and found various articles in the paper about a Nick Heaton being arrested a couple of times, but it might not be the same man; I couldn't find photos of him to match with his driver's license photo. I also found out that there is a Nick Heaton who sells used cars. Ava continued, "But definitely most of Camille's incoming calls were from the woman doctor. There were also calls listed from the hospital to Camille's cell phone."

"Strange. I wonder who that woman was that Camille was arguing with. Would it have been the doctor, or Leah Miller, or someone else? I wonder whether Camille was sick?"

"Why would she argue with her doctor if she was sick? She could have been one of the doctor's volunteers."

"I don't know. Good work finding all that out. Be sure to thank your friend for me." Ettie took a moment to take a deep breath. "Come with me to the hospital. I've got to see what's happening with Elsa-May. I'm worried about her."

WHEN ETTIE and Ava got to the hospital, Ettie was surprised to be directed to a room on the top floor. They found the room and walked in to see that Elsa-May was sharing a room with three other women. Elsa-May was at the far wall near the window.

"Have you had the tests yet?" was the first thing Ettie asked when she stood next to Elsa-May's bed.

Elsa-May smiled at Ava. "Nice to see you, Ava."

"You feeling okay?"

Elsa-May nodded. "Fine." She looked at Ettie. "I've had an ultrasound, but they couldn't tell anything. They said the test was inconclusive and now I have to stay in while they do another test. Looks like I'll be in overnight."

"You'll need some things if you're going to be in overnight. I'll go home and bring some things to you."

"*Nee.* I'll wear the hospital gown. It doesn't bother me. I've got everything I need. Don't exhaust yourself rushing around."

"What kind of test will they do, Elsa-May?" Ava asked.

"They call it a venogram. They shoot dye into me through a catheter and then X-ray me."

Ava winced. "Sounds like it might be painful."

"I hope not," Elsa-May said. "I don't have much of a choice but to go ahead and do it."

"They can't do it today?" Ava asked.

Elsa-May shook her head. "They're doing it tomorrow. I have to fast for hours before they do the X-ray."

"Well, I guess I don't need to bring you any food, then," Ettie said.

"Take my mind off things and tell me what you've found out," Elsa-May said.

Ettie and Ava told her what they knew so far about the people on the list Ettie had gotten from Kelly.

"This Judith Mackelvanner is a neurologist?"

"*Jah,*" Ettie and Ava said at the same time.

"Neurology is something to do with the brain, I believe," Elsa-May said. "And from what you know so far, do you think Camille might have been arguing with Judith or Leah?"

"We've no idea; it might have been neither of them," Ava said.

"What reason would she have for arguing with a neurologist?" Elsa-May asked.

Ettie was silent while she thought. "It could have been something personal. Just because this Judith Mackelvanner is a doctor doesn't mean that the argument was about something medical."

"I suppose it could've been about anything." Ava chewed on the end of her thumbnail.

"Could she have been Nehemiah's doctor?" Ettie suggested.

"I don't think so. He died from heart disease and this doctor studies the brain," Elsa-May said.

Ava turned to Ettie. "Why don't you ask Mildred if she's heard of Dr. Judith Mackelvanner?"

"That's a good idea, Ava. A good idea indeed. I'll take you to your place, and then I'll have the taxi continue to Mildred's *haus*."

"Okay."

Ettie turned to Elsa-May. "Are you sure you don't need anything?"

"*Jah*, I'm sure. Don't tell anyone I'm in the hospital. I don't want anyone to worry, and I don't want visitors fussing about."

"Okay." Ettie leaned over and rubbed her sister's arm. "You'll be in my prayers."

Elsa-May breathed out heavily and closed her eyes as she said, *"Denke."*

Ettie turned to Ava. "Come on, then."

"Bye, Elsa-May," Ava said.

"Goodbye," Elsa-May said without opening her eyes.

CHAPTER 10

hen Ettie and Ava approached Ava's place, Ettie was surprised to see Jeremiah's buggy. She looked closer and saw Jeremiah standing near his horse.

"My goodness. What's he doing here? I wonder if Elsa-May saw him and let him know I wanted him to do some jobs at the *haus*."

"I think he's here to see me, Ettie."

Ettie frowned and looked at Ava only to see her face flush crimson. "He is? That's wonderful news."

Ava gave a little giggle. "It's not like that. We're just friends and that's all."

"*Jah,* that's what everyone says. That's what I told my parents when my late husband and I were secretly courting."

Ava shook her head.

When Ava got out of the taxi, Ettie said, "Say hello to Jeremiah for me and tell him I've got some work for him, when he's got some spare time." Ettie smiled and resisted teasing Ava. Ettie called after her, "That'll save me talking to him on Sunday."

Five minutes later, Ettie was at Mildred's house.

After Ettie told Mildred about Elsa-May being in the hospital and asked her to keep quiet about it, she inquired about Jacob.

Mildred answered her. "The lawyer's only just left. He asked Jacob a lot of questions. Anyway, Jacob's very tired, but he's out back now fixing fences. He's a hard worker. We've saved geld with Jacob being able to work. Camille couldn't work on the farm; all she could do was organize the workers and she didn't do that very well at all, so Nehemiah said."

"*Jah*, I suppose you would save a lot on labor now that Jacob can be so hands-on. The police haven't been back around?"

"*Nee*."

"Tell me, Mildred, have you ever heard of a Dr. Mackelvanner?"

Mildred's eyebrows drew together. "I can't say for certain that I have, but the name does sound a little familiar. Was she one of the doctors that Nehemiah went to see?"

"I'm not sure. He saw a few different doctors?"

"*Jah*, he went to one who referred him to others; all of them tried to find out exactly what was wrong with him. His symptoms were fairly general. He went downhill so quickly."

Ettie poked a finger under her prayer *kapp* and scratched her head. "This woman, Dr. Mackelvanner, specializes in brain disorders. Do you know anyone afflicted with anything like that?"

"Only Mary."

"Mary?" Ettie hadn't figured that the doctor might have had something to do with Mary and her condition.

Mildred nodded. "Nehemiah told me that Mary had mental problems. I always thought that Camille suffered the same thing."

"So Mary would've seen a doctor."

"What's all this about, Ettie?"

"I'm following up on a few things that might be able to help Jacob. They seem unrelated at the moment, but I'm hoping they'll all piece together at the end."

"Thank you for helping. You've been *wunderbaar*. I couldn't be certain who the doctor was that Mary saw, but Nehemiah did say that Mary had some kind of mental disorder and that's all I know. He said that not long after she started having violent episodes, she was gone in a matter of months."

Ettie thought back to Mary as she'd known her many years ago, and at the time, she'd had no idea that Mary was sick. "Would Jacob know more about it?"

"*Nee*, he was only a young *bu* when Mary went home to be with *Gott*. Not unless his *vadder* told him something of it in later years, but I don't know."

"That's possible."

"Except Nehemiah wasn't much of a talker."

Ettie pushed her lips and nodded. Many of the Amish men weren't good at talking. Her own father had to be asked about his childhood and only then would he tell her stories, whereas her mother had often told her stories about how things were when she was growing up.

"Stay for lunch, Ettie. Jacob will be home and you can ask him yourself."

"*Denke*, I'll do that."

When Jacob came home, Ettie had a chance to ask him about his mother's illness.

"*Jah*, I didn't know when I was young she was sick, but I found out when I was older that my *mudder* had something called Creutzfeldt-Jakob disease. I was upset that it kind of shared my name."

Ettie frowned. "I've never heard of such a thing."

"It's a degenerative disease of the central nervous system, apparently. I looked into it."

"That sounds awful. Was she treated by a neurologist?"

"I don't know. I couldn't get much information out of *Dat* about the whole thing. He didn't like to talk about her much. It made him too upset."

"She was your *mudder;* you had a right to ask as many questions as you wanted to and have your questions answered," Mildred said.

Jacob nodded and the corners of his mouth twitched. "Why do you ask, Ettie?"

"I'm following up on a few things." Ettie figured she should tell him the truth. "In point of actual fact, I've reason to believe that your *schweschder* had many conversations with a doctor from the hospital. I found out today when I was visiting Elsa-May..."

Jacob interrupted, "Elsa-May's in the hospital?"

"Don't worry about her, she's okay, and don't let

anyone know she's there. She's just having some tests. Anyway, I found out that the doctor is a woman, and she's also a neurologist. I was just wondering if she might have had anything to do with your *mudder's* treatment."

"I wouldn't be able to tell you. Is the doctor old?"

"I haven't seen her in person, but I'll find out how old she'd be. I saw a photo and she didn't look very old, maybe around forty or so."

"Anyone who treated my *mudder* would have to be around sixty I'd guess."

Ettie knew she'd slipped up. She should've had Ava check the ages of the people. Dr. Mackelvanner seemed as though she'd be too young to have treated Mary Esh. Ava's friend from the DMV would've had the birth dates recorded on the system.

Ettie turned to Mildred. "You said someone told you they saw Camille in town arguing with a woman. Did they say what the woman looked like?"

"A woman with long dark hair, an *Englischer.* That's all they said."

"Really?"

Mildred nodded. "That's right."

"This doctor has long dark hair."

"So my *schweschder* had many conversations with this doctor and she was seen arguing with a woman who fits the doctor's description? What does any of this have to do with me? Do you think the doctor you're asking about murdered Camille?"

"I don't know. I'm trying to find out who Camille was talking to and why. That could go a long way to finding out if she'd upset anyone enough for them to want her gone."

"I'm sorry, Ettie. I don't mean to be irritable, or ungrateful. *Denke* for helping, but I don't think there's anything you can do. I'll just have to wait, hope, and trust in *Gott* that the police give me the all clear."

"And they will because you didn't do anything," Mildred said.

Jacob smiled at Mildred.

It was getting late in the day, and Ettie figured that she shouldn't press anything further since both Jacob and Mildred were under a lot of pressure. The best thing she could do was go and see Detective Kelly. He'd be able to find out about the doctor even if he had to go and ask the doctor how she knew Camille.

After Jacob went back to his farm work and Ettie finished helping Mildred with washing the dishes, Ettie made her way back to the police station.

The officer at the front desk must have recognized her; because before Ettie said a word, he said, "Detective Kelly?"

Ettie smiled. "Yes, thank you."

"Have a seat. I'll call him."

Ettie did as she was instructed and sat on the wooden bench in the waiting area. She'd barely sat down when she saw Kelly walking toward her. When their eyes met he smiled and told her, with a wave of his hand, to come into his office.

Once she was sitting opposite him, he asked, "What can I do for you today? By the way, thank Elsa-May for the food, would you?"

"You ate it?"

"Of course I did. I haven't had a good meal like that in a long time."

Ettie smiled. "I was the one who cooked it, but it was Elsa-May's idea when I told her about the donuts you ate for lunch."

"I am going to make an effort, and try to eat healthier."

"Glad to hear it."

"Now, what can I do for you?"

"From the list of numbers you gave me, I found out that most of the incoming and outgoing calls were from the same person. She's a doctor at the hospital. Sometimes she'd call Camille from her cell phone and other times there were calls to Camille's cell phone from the number at the hospital. Then there were calls from Camille to the doctor's mobile, but Camille never called the hospital – not within the time-frame that the list you gave me was constructed."

Detective Kelly frowned. "Was Camille sick or something?"

"I don't know, but the doctor was working with volunteers so maybe Camille was one of those. The other thing I had to tell you was that two people saw Camille in town arguing with a woman who had long dark hair, and Dr. Mackelvanner has long dark hair."

Kelly rubbed his nose.

"I did have a thought," Ettie said.

"What was it?"

"The doctor is a neurologist. I thought their contact could be something to do with Camille's mother's death. Her mother died of some rare condition, and I believe a doctor who had the same qualifications as Dr. Mackel-vanner would've treated her. It's a big coincidence, isn't it?"

"I'm not following you."

Ettie squirmed in her seat. She wasn't certain what it all meant, and was hoping Kelly might be able to shed some light on it for her. "I was hoping that you might be able to question this doctor and see how she knew Camille."

"I don't see that it matters." When Ettie glared at him, he said, "I'll make a note of it. I don't have the time to follow it up right now. I'm glad you came in."

"You are?"

"Yes. I've got some bad news."

Ettie braced herself, hoping it wasn't about Jacob. "You're glad I came in so you can give me bad news? I'm not glad I came in if all you have for me is bad news."

"The bullets found in Camille's apartment match one of the firearms we took from the Esh house. I'm waiting on the warrant for Jacob Esh's arrest to come through."

Ettie gasped and covered her mouth. "No! It can't be."

"I appreciate your loyalty, Mrs. Smith, but sometimes people can fool us. Just because he was born into an Amish family doesn't mean he's a saint who is not capable of murder."

"He didn't do it, and I'll prove it one way or another."

Kelly raised his eyebrows. "I suppose it's my fault for getting you involved in all this, and for that, I'm sorry."

"I dare say I would've gotten involved anyway once I found out that you arrested the wrong man."

"We've got enough evidence to arrest him."

"The gun?"

"Yes, the gun." He rose to his feet. "I don't want to appear rude, but I've got a lot on my plate."

Ettie put both hands on his desk and pushed herself to her feet. "Good day, Detective." Ettie walked out of his office, not sure what to do. Should she warn Mildred what was about to happen? Mildred would be so upset, but as Elsa-May had said to her, Mildred wasn't without people she could call on. Mildred had a telephone in her barn and she could call someone whenever she needed. Ettie got a taxi home, had the taxi wait while she collected some fresh clothes and a nightdress for Elsa-May, and then continued on to the hospital. Elsa-May had picked a bad time to get sick.

CHAPTER 11

*S*upported by pillows in her upright position in the hospital bed, Elsa-May smiled when Ettie came into the hospital room. "I'll be glad to get out of this place. They keep asking me what my name is. I keep telling them it's written there." She pointed to the name behind her.

Ettie giggled. "They're trying to find out if you're still in your right mind."

"They should find a better way of doing it, then. I'm not a three-year-old. And all the nurses speak loudly to me as though I'm deaf."

"I know. I remember that from when I was in hospital with pneumonia." Ettie placed Elsa-May's clothes in a drawer of the nightstand. "I've brought some things for you." Ettie then slumped on the edge of Elsa-May's bed.

"Well, what happened this afternoon when you left here? You look like you've had the wind knocked out of you."

"A lot happened. The short version of it is that Kelly's probably at this very moment arresting Jacob."

"Really?"

Ettie nodded.

"That's bad news."

"He said one of Jacob's rifles, or some type of gun, was a match with the bullets found in Camille's apartment. That's not all I found out today."

"What else?"

Ettie told Elsa-May about the doctor whom Camille had often been speaking to, and the possibility that the doctor might have been the woman Camille had been seen arguing with.

"Did you tell Kelly that?"

"I did, but he didn't seem interested. He said he'd look into it later, but I'm sure he only said that to keep me quiet or make me happy. *Nee,* not to make me happy. He wouldn't care if he made anyone happy or not. He said it just for something to say, I'm certain of that."

"I suppose he had his mind on making the arrest. Didn't he say he was up for a promotion?"

Ettie nodded. "I hope he doesn't let that cloud his judgment over whether Jacob is innocent or not."

"Looks like it's too late for that if he's gone ahead with the warrant. At least Jacob knows a lawyer now. Is he any good?"

"The lawyer?"

Elsa-May nodded.

"He's a little odd, and very young. I don't know if he's good, but he did get Jacob out of the police station pretty fast; perhaps he is good. He was questioning Jacob today so he does seem enthusiastic."

"Does that doctor you were talking about work at this hospital?"

"According to the phone records she does."

"Now, what about that man from next door to the Eshes' property, the one who wanted to buy the farm? With Camille dead, and if Jacob goes to jail, that would leave Mildred with the farm, and she'd most likely sell to him."

"That's right. He could've gone into the Eshes' home, taken one of Jacob's rifles and shot at Camille, and then put it back. He could've killed Camille, and then because of the bullet matching Jacob's gun it would have looked like Jacob made an attempt on his sister's life." Ettie tapped on her chin. "The only thing is that Mildred's at home all the time, so he wouldn't have had a chance to take the gun and then put it back."

"There's the gatherings she goes to every second Sunday, and she goes out to the knitting circle when it isn't held at her *haus*. What if he planted a gun there and it wasn't Jacob's gun after all? Did anyone think of that?"

"*Nee*, I don't think they did, and I wonder if they even checked the prints on the gun. I suppose they would've."

"Yes. I'd expect so," Elsa-May said.

Ettie continued, "Mildred wouldn't know what gun was what. She said there were quite a few guns, and some were Nehemiah's. Also Mildred did say that the neighbor keeps an eye on the place. While I was visiting Mildred he was just standing there staring at their *haus*."

"Now what about Camille? How do you think she knows the doctor?"

"Jacob said his mother had some kind of mental illness and was treated for some disorder or other. She could very well have been seen by a neurologist."

"What illness was it?"

"I can't remember. I should've written it down. It was a strange name that I'd never come across before."

"What did Camille do when she was away from the community? I assumed she would've worked somewhere. Could she have met the doctor while she was working?"

"From what I heard, Camille worked at a winery. Something to do with making the wine."

"Stomping on grapes?" Elsa-May said with a laugh.

Ettie smiled. "Perhaps something in the office, since she told Nehemiah she had management experience."

"Should you find this doctor and talk to her?" Elsa-May asked.

"*Ach, nee.* I wouldn't like to. Detective Kelly should be the one to do that. It might not have anything to do with anything."

"Perhaps," Elsa-May said. "And it doesn't sound likely that a doctor would've killed Camille. Doctors are supposed to try to prolong lives, not cut them short."

"*Jah.* Intriguing, though, isn't it? The woman's not an ordinary doctor, and they had so many conversations."

"Perhaps Camille was sick."

"No one mentioned that might be the case. Certainly Jacob or Mildred weren't aware of any illness."

"Was Mary's illness something that might have been passed on?"

"I don't know why I didn't think of that. What was it now? It was something or other Jacob disease."

"Creutzfeldt-Jakob disease?"

"That was it. How do you know about it?"

"Yes, I think it can be passed on in some cases."

"How do you know about it?" Ettie repeated.

"It's one of the diseases that there's no cure for. I remember reading about it and I can't remember where. When people get it, I'm certain they go downhill quickly. I think, as I've already said, it might be something that could be passed on. We'd have to find out for certain."

"I wonder if Camille had the disease and didn't tell anyone. If so, why would she be arguing with her doctor?"

"Perhaps it wasn't her doctor she was arguing with. It could've been someone else," Elsa-May suggested. "Although the description did match the doctor. Anyway, you'd better go and see how Mildred is. Don't worry about me; I'm okay. I still remember who I am."

"Are you sure? I can stay with you longer. I don't want to run into Detective Kelly, and I certainly don't want to arrive there before he's been out to Mildred's *haus.*"

Elsa-May glanced at the phone on the nightstand beside her. "Why don't you call Mildred? Tell her you're going to come there. You'll soon find out if the detective's been there."

Ettie made the call and found out that Detective Kelly had arrested Jacob, and they'd just left. When Ettie hung up the receiver, she turned to Elsa-May. "She's near hysterical. I told her to phone the lawyer and that I'd be right over."

"*Jah,* I heard what you said."

"I do hate leaving you. I'd like to sit by you longer."

"*Nee,* don't be silly; you go. There'll be someone coming in soon asking me my name. I might have some fun with them this time. I'll tell them I don't know my name." Elsa-May chuckled.

Ettie wagged a finger at her sister. "Don't you do that."

"Okay, I won't." Elsa-May settled herself back into the pillow and closed her eyes. "I'll have a little sleep before the next meal comes 'round."

"*Nee,* you can't eat, remember?"

Elsa-May chuckled. "I was just testing to see if you were listening to me."

"You can't be too sick."

"Tell that to the doctor on your way out, would you?"

Ettie patted Elsa-May on her shoulder. "I'll come back and see you in the morning."

"*Denke,*" Elsa-May said, without opening her eyes.

CHAPTER 12

"*E*ttie, I'm so glad you're here."

"Did you call the lawyer?"

Mildred nodded. "*Jah*, he said he'd go straight to the police station."

"That's good of him." Ettie looked Mildred up and down. "You don't look as poorly as you sounded on the phone."

"I prayed and left things up to *Gott*. I know Jacob's innocent no matter what the police say. They'll find that out soon enough."

"That's the way," Ettie said, thinking she should've stayed with Elsa-May.

"The lawyer said Jacob would probably get bail, so if he does he'll be out in the morning just as soon as he can go before a judge."

"Very good."

"Ettie, you don't look well."

Ettie put her fingertips to her face only to feel that her

cheeks were burning. "I've been busy over the last couple of days."

Mildred looped her arm through Ettie's. "Come sit down and have a cup of tea. Would you stay for dinner?"

"I'd love to stay, *denke*." Ettie hadn't given any thought to dinner and with Elsa-May in the hospital, she most likely would've only eaten fruit when she got home.

After an early dinner, Mildred insisted on driving Ettie home rather than her getting a taxi. After Mildred hitched the horse and buggy, she said, "Why don't you just stay the night? Elsa-May's in the hospital and I'll be alone too."

"All right. I will." Ettie gave a little laugh. "Now we've hitched the buggy for nothing." Ettie patted the fine chestnut gelding on his neck. The horse turned his head and Ettie rubbed his soft nose. "You're a beauty," Ettie said to the horse.

"It doesn't hurt for me to practice hitching the buggy. If anything happens to Jacob I'll be on my own. I've never been on my own. I went straight from my *mudder* and *vadder's haus* to Nehemiah's."

"Don't talk like that. We have to stay steadfast in trusting *Gott*."

Mildred nodded. "I'm trying, but sometimes I let the worry overtake me."

"Let's put the horse back in the paddock. Then you and I can sleep."

That night, Ettie stayed up much longer than usual while listening to Mildred tell stories of when she and Nehemiah were courting. Ettie felt a little sad for her. It didn't seem like there had been any real courtship; it wasn't a romantic time for Mildred. It sounded to Ettie like Nehemiah hadn't gotten over Mary's death. It seemed more a marriage of convenience for Nehemiah, but Mildred obviously hadn't seen things like that, or if she had she wasn't admitting it. Nehemiah had needed someone to look after his children while he worked the farm and Mildred was glad to finally be someone's wife and have an instant family.

"Camille couldn't have remembered Mary very well. Why do you think that she never truly accepted you as her *mudder?*"

Mildred heaved a deep sigh. "I don't know where I went wrong with her, what I could've done differently. Nehemiah stopped talking about Mary so the *kinner* could adjust better to me. I didn't want them to forget her or anything. I just wanted to do the job that Mary would've wanted me to do; to look after and care for them properly."

Ettie yawned and saw that it was nearly eleven. "Excuse me. I think my old body's telling me I need some sleep."

"Jah, me too. Who knows what tomorrow will bring?"

THE NEXT MORNING, Ettie heard the front door shut loudly. She opened her eyes and looked around, taking a moment to realize that she was in Mildred's house. Then she heard someone bustling around in the kitchen downstairs. Ettie poured some water into a bowl and splashed it on her face before she changed out of the borrowed nightgown and into her dress. Once she'd slipped her over-apron on, she wound her hair up on her head and placed her prayer *kapp* over the top. She made the bed and then headed downstairs.

"You awake already, Mildred?" Ettie said as she walked into the kitchen.

"It's half past nine."

Ettie opened her mouth in shock. "Is it? I never sleep this late." Ettie looked out the window to see a gray sky. "Usually the light wakes me. Looks like we might be in for rain."

"Have a seat, Ettie, and I'll make you some breakfast."

Ettie smiled, glad to have someone look after her for a change. With Elsa-May's leg being so bad for weeks, Ettie had been left to do all the cooking and all the chores.

"I was making the bread this morning when I heard the phone in the barn ringing."

"Did you make it there in time to answer?"

"*Jah*. It was the lawyer. He was saying something about them having Jacob's fingerprints somewhere."

"Where?"

"I couldn't really hear – the phone had a crackling in it. He said he'd either call me back or come here. He's hoping to get Jacob out this morning. Could you wait with me, Ettie?"

"Of course I can."

Mildred smiled at Ettie while she poured hot water into a china teapot. Ettie did want to see how Elsa-May was, but she figured Elsa-May wouldn't be ready to go home until the afternoon.

It wasn't long after they'd finished breakfast when

they heard a car. Both ladies looked out the window to see the lawyer's car heading toward the house.

"He's got Jacob with him," Mildred said.

"*Jah*, I can see someone sitting next to the driver."

Mildred rushed to the door and waited on the porch for the car to pull up. Just as the car stopped, the rain pelted down.

Jacob got out of the car and Mildred ran and wrapped her arms around him. He put his arm around her and then they ran back to the cover of the porch.

"Everything's okay, *Mamm*," Jacob said.

Ettie stood in the doorway. She saw the lawyer get out of the car and hurry toward them. When he stood next to Jacob, he wiped the rain off his suit and said, "The latest is…"

Mildred interrupted, "Do come inside and we can sit. I can barely hear anything with this rain."

Once they were all sitting in the living room, the lawyer said, "They claim to have found Jacob's fingerprints in Camille's apartment."

"And I was never in her apartment," Jacob said to Mildred.

"Jacob's prints were on two glasses in her apartment, and one of the glasses, the one we know Camille had drunk out of, had remnants of poison in it."

"The poison that killed her?" Mildred asked.

Claymore nodded. "One of the poisons. She had two in her system."

Mildred gasped and clutched at her stomach.

"We don't have to talk about this now," Claymore said.

Mildred shook her head. "No, it's all right. Continue."

"Very well. Things aren't looking good for Jacob with his prints on the glasses, and the bullets."

Ettie noticed that the lawyer swallowed hard and exchanged worried glances with Jacob.

"Is there more, Mr. Cartwright?" Ettie asked.

The lawyer raised his eyebrows and then looked back at Jacob.

"You might as well tell 'em," Jacob said.

"One of the poisons that killed Camille was found in your barn, Mrs. Esh. Ethylene glycol. It's a painful death, so I'm told."

Mildred's hand flew to her mouth. "My barn? What would poison be doing in my barn?"

"Many people keep it. It's a common thing a lot of people would have for their vehicles."

"If it's common, couldn't anyone have used that poison?" Ettie asked.

"The thing is the formula has been changed in the last few years. It used to taste sweet and now they're making it taste awful." He looked at Mildred. "The one in Camille's system was the old formula, same as the one found in your barn."

"I heard she died from an overdose of some kind of sleeping pills," Mildred said to the lawyer.

The lawyer gave a nod. "They ran a second lot of tests and found she had both in her system. Traces of the sleeping pills were found in the glass – they are assuming they were dissolved in some kind of drink."

Detective Kelly must have known that, and he'd held back that information from her. Ettie decided that this would be the last time she'd help him.

"There's a lot of evidence against me," Jacob said, looking at Mildred. "I didn't do it."

Mildred nodded. "Why would we have poison here?"

"The poison in question is used in motor vehicles as a coolant," Claymore said.

"We don't have motor vehicles."

"Claymore looked it up and found that the coolant can also be used to protect some metals, or as a solvent. *Dat* probably had a bottle in the barn to preserve some metal, maybe the old buggy his *vadder* had. He was always tinkering with it."

Ettie pushed herself to her feet. "Why don't I make everyone some tea?"

"I can't stay long," Claymore said.

"Tea won't take long," Ettie said before she hurried to the kitchen. While she was there, Ettie could still hear their conversation. She turned on the stove, filled the pot and placed it on the heating plate. Then she set about placing teacups and saucers onto a tray. She knew Mildred always kept sugar cookies in a jar in the larder. Ettie found the cookies and placed them on a plate.

Claymore told Mildred that the evidence was circumstantial. It would be normal for Camille to have her brother's fingerprints in her apartment. "Anyone could have had access to some ethylene glycol. It's something many people keep."

Ettie carried the tray of cookies and teacups out to them while she waited for the pot to boil.

"What about the gun? Was the gun in question left in the house?" Ettie asked.

Jacob nodded, and Mildred said, "The guns are always

left in the *haus*. Nehemiah always kept the guns in the *haus,* never in the barn."

"And did they show you the gun in question?"

Jacob nodded. "It was one of *Dat's*. They asked me if I recognized it."

"I'd better check to see if the water's boiled." Ettie hurried back to the kitchen and poured the boiling water into the teapot.

After the lawyer left Mildred's house, Ettie was tired and left for her home.

When the taxi stopped at her home, Ettie was pleased she'd be able to have a rest before going back to the hospital. Just as she opened her gate, she saw Bernie, the neighbor walking his dog.

"Hello, Ettie."

"Hello." Ettie leaned down to pat his dog. "It's a nice day for a walk."

He pushed his hat back on his head. "Where's Elsa-May? I don't often see you out and about on your own."

"Elsa-May's in the hospital. Nothing serious. She'll be home anytime."

"Ah. I see. Well, I'd better keep going."

Ettie headed toward her front door hoping Elsa-May wouldn't be mad at her for telling Bernie she was in the hospital. She had asked Ettie not to tell anyone, but Bernie asked, so what was she to do?

After a rest, Ettie headed to the hospital, hoping Elsa-May wouldn't be mad at her for leaving her alone for so long.

Ettie walked in to the hospital room and saw Elsa-May

reading the bible that had been in the drawer next to her bed. Elsa-May smiled when she saw Ettie walk in.

"Are you ready to come home yet?" Ettie asked.

"I don't think I'll be able to leave until tomorrow. I've had some kind of reaction to the dye." Elsa-May lifted the sheet to reveal a very red, swollen leg.

"Agh. That doesn't look good. Does it hurt?"

"Funny thing is, it doesn't hurt anymore than it did before. The test today was uncomfortable, but at least I can eat again. They've given me the all clear."

"You don't have a clot?"

"*Nee,* I don't."

"That's *wunderbaar.* What caused your leg pain, though?"

"That, they haven't found out yet. The doctor from this hospital also said something about me having to lose weight, and that would improve circulation. Maybe that's why my leg's been hurting." Elsa-May pushed the sheet back over her leg and Ettie straightened the end of the sheet.

"Shouldn't you let the air get to your leg?" Ettie asked.

"*Nee,* the breeze of the air-conditioning irritates it. Tell me what the latest news is."

Ettie told Elsa-May all that had been said at Mildred's house.

"The only way I can figure that Jacob's gun was used was if someone had deliberately tried to make it look like Jacob did it. They would've had to sneak into the house, use the gun, and then place the gun back in the house. Or, as I've said before, was it Jacob's gun in the first place?"

"I asked Jacob about that. He said it *was* one of his *vadder's* old guns." Ettie continued, "The lawyer says it's all circumstantial evidence. All the same, I think the lawyer's worried, and I know Jacob is dreadfully concerned to the point of being sick. He tries to be brave but I can see the worry in his face."

"Well, hello."

Both women looked in the direction of the familiar voice.

"Detective Crowley, it's so nice to see you." Ettie was overjoyed to see him and tried to contain her excitement. Now they might get someone to help them, or at least listen to them.

The detective glanced around the hospital room and moved toward Elsa-May's bed.

"How did you know I was here?" Elsa-May asked as Crowley walked further into the room.

"One of your neighbors told me where to find you."

Elsa-May glared at Ettie. "Ettie, I asked you not to tell anyone I was in the hospital."

"I was walking out the front gate and Bernie was walking his dog. He asked where you were and I couldn't lie."

Elsa-May sighed.

Crowley said, "I heard an Amish man was arrested for the murder of his sister. I figured you would know the people involved."

Elsa-May looked at Ettie. "Pull the curtains, would you?" Ettie pulled the curtains around the bed to give them privacy from the three other patients in the room.

"We do know them," Ettie said in a low voice, hoping that he was there to help them. Now they might finally be able to help Jacob if the former detective was going to be on their side.

Crowley said, "I thought of both of you as soon as I heard."

"Thank you," Elsa-May said.

"Do you know the family well?" Crowley asked.

"Yes," Ettie said.

"Mildred, the mother – well, the stepmother – is in my knitting circle," Elsa-May said.

"Any chance of you coming out of retirement?" Ettie asked, staring at him and hoping he'd say that he'd help.

He frowned at Ettie. "Why? Is there a problem?"

Ettie and Elsa-May filled the detective in on what had happened. Ettie finished up by saying, "I'm not happy with Detective Kelly and how he tricked me in the beginning."

"I can understand how you feel about that. From what you said they've got pretty strong evidence against the young man."

"Be that as it may, he's innocent. I know he didn't do it," Ettie said.

Crowley rubbed his chin.

"Can you see what you can find out for us?" Elsa-May asked. "It's hard for Ettie with me in the hospital. She's been doing a lot of rushing here and there, and it's not easy at her age."

Normally Ettie would've taken offense at Elsa-May's reference to her age since Elsa-May was the older of the two, but she didn't mind at all if it prompted Crowley to help them.

"I'll see what I can do. I'll go straight in there. I visit

everyone there every so often so it won't look like I'm there on an information-gathering expedition."

"Even though you are," Elsa-May chortled.

"Do you expect to be in here for long?" Crowley asked Elsa-May.

"I'm hoping to be out tomorrow."

"It's not possible that he can be found guilty if he didn't do it, is it?" Ettie asked before she thought the question through. She knew, of course, innocent people had been found guilty in the past.

"It does happen more often than you'd think. Some people have served long prison sentences and now, with the new DNA testing constantly evolving, they're finding out they were innocent."

Just then a nurse poked her head through the curtains. "I thought I heard voices. Visiting hours is over."

"Visiting hours are over," Elsa-May corrected her.

"Yes, that's right," the nurse grumbled while staring at the visitors, not realizing that Elsa-May had corrected her.

Crowley said, "I'm sorry. I wasn't aware there were restrictions."

Ettie took a step toward the nurse. "I'm her sister. I find it hard to get here in visiting hours."

"Well, I'll go and see some other patients and I'll be back in ten minutes to check on the patient."

"Thank you," Crowley said.

The nurse walked out.

"Can I drive you home, Ettie?"

Ettie's face lit up. "Yes, thank you. That'll save me getting a taxi."

"Off you go; don't mind me. I don't want you to get

into trouble when Nurse Grisly comes back," Elsa-May said, laughing.

"Is that her real name?" Ettie asked.

Elsa-May chuckled again. "Yes, it is. I know because she signs my chart."

"You look at your chart?" Crowley asked, picking up the chart hanging on the end of the bed.

"Why not? It's my chart. I can't make head or tail of it, but I still read it. Hopefully they'll say I can go home tomorrow. The doctor will see me in the morning when he does his rounds."

CHAPTER 13

n the way home, Ettie told Crowley as many details as she knew about Camille and Jacob.

When he stopped the car, Crowley said, "From what you said, Kelly's looking at a promotion. He'll be trying to get all the help he can so he'll look good."

"I think he only wants the kind of help that'll make Jacob look more guilty. He might not like help if you're trying to find a way to prove he's innocent."

"There's only one way to find out." Crowley glanced at his wristwatch. "Hopefully he's working late."

"You're going there right now?"

Crowley nodded.

"I'm concerned that Kelly knows about the argument Camille was seen having with a woman and yet he's done nothing to find out who she might be," Ettie said.

"And two different people told you that, you say?"

"That's right. The man next door, what was his name again? That's right, his last name was Bradshaw. I'm certain it was Ronald Bradshaw. And then someone told Camille's stepmother that they saw Camille in town arguing with a lady with long black hair."

"And you think that woman is the doctor?"

Ettie nodded. "She is a doctor." Ettie was pretty sure that she'd told him enough details, and he understood enough to find out a few things to help Jacob. Crowley believed her based solely on her word that Jacob wasn't guilty. Unless he was tricking her like Detective Kelly had. *Nee!* She shook the thought from her mind. Crowley had always been straight with them. He wasn't deceptive at all, unlike Kelly.

Once Crowley had driven away, Ettie unlocked her front door and pushed it open. She wasn't used to coming home to an empty house.

For dinner she ate a couple of pieces of fruit and then sat down on the couch to do some more needlework. A few minutes after she'd begun, she looked at the wooden chair that Elsa-May usually sat in. Without Elsa-May knitting while she sewed it seemed to be a waste of time and not as interesting. Ettie sighed and bundled the needlework up and pushed it to one end of the couch.

She closed her eyes and before long her mind drifted to Jacob and the evidence that was stacked against him. She hoped that Kelly would allow Crowley to help, just like he had last time.

A sudden knock on the door made Ettie jump. "Who could that be?" she muttered.

She opened the door to see Ava. Ettie immediately felt bad that she hadn't visited her and kept her up to date with what was going on. "Ava, come in. Can I get you something?"

"*Nee*, I'm fine. It's not been long since I had dinner."

"Come and sit down."

Once the two of them were sitting down together, Ettie told Ava everything that had happened since she'd seen her last.

"It would be interesting to know more about that doctor."

"The only way we could find out if Camille knew her because she was sick is if someone looked up Camille's medical records." Ettie clicked her fingers. "I should've mentioned that to Crowley. I told him everything I could remember, but I was trying to tell him all the facts about the evidence. I did tell him about the woman Camille was seen arguing with."

Ava's eyes glazed over.

"What is it, Ava?"

"Oh, I was just thinking how we'd be able to find out about Camille's medical history."

"I don't think we can, can we? I haven't been able to think of a way, not with the patient-privacy regulations these days."

"Hmmm, I'll give it some thought."

"Is there any way we can look up the records on the hospital computer if we both go and see Elsa-May tomorrow morning? You distract the nurse while I look on her computer."

Ettie giggled. "*Nee*, we can't do that. The patient files on the computer might not be open, anyway."

"Well, I think it'd be worth a try."

"There'll have to be another way. Anyway, we're putting a lot of store on this woman having something to do with Camille's death. She might not have anything to do with it at all. I think we'd do better to consider who would've taken a gun out of Jacob's *haus*, shot at Camille in her apartment, then placed the gun back in Jacob's *haus*."

"Either Jacob did do it, or it looks like someone wanted it to look like he did it."

Ettie was painfully curious to know more about Camille's life. "Mildred did talk about a friend of Camille's. I can't remember exactly, but I'm fairly certain Camille still kept in contact with an *Englischer*. We should look into the girl who left the community, Leah Miller."

"Whoever did kill Camille had planned it carefully. It wasn't something they rushed into. Who has Camille's cell phone?"

Ettie's eyes opened wide. "I'm not certain, but if the police didn't take it, maybe Mildred would let us take a look at it."

"*Jah*, there could be texts and voice messages."

"Surely the police would have taken it in as evidence. Or it might be still at her apartment."

"Would they have taken it?" Ava asked. "They got her phone records."

"As soon as I see what's happening with Elsa-May in the hospital tomorrow, I'll go over and visit Mildred. They could be letting Elsa-May out tomorrow. It would've been today, only she had some kind of reaction to something they gave her."

"Do you want me to come with you?"

"Nee, I don't want to bother you to go to the hospital, but I would like you to come with me when I go to Mildred's *haus."*

"I'd be happy to. What if I come here at twelve? Do you think you'd be back from the hospital by then?"

"Why don't I give you a call when I'm leaving the hospital? We have to wait until the doctor does his rounds, and that could be anytime in the morning. I wouldn't want you waiting here a long time. *Ach,* there's no phone at your place."

"That's okay. I'll go to my *mudder's haus* and you can call me there."

"Denke, Ava. That should work out well."

NEXT MORNING, Ettie was back at the hospital with Elsa-May.

"Have you had a good night?"

"Nee. My leg was hurting all night and now they say my blood pressure is up. Why wouldn't it be up, having to stay in this place for days?"

"You do look a little pale."

"That's because I've been here for days with no fresh air or sunshine. It's not a healthy place to be."

Ettie chuckled. "It is if you're sick."

"You don't like hospitals yourself, Ettie."

"That's true. I don't know if anyone would be able to make me stay in one ever again. Crowley was going to see Kelly last night, but I don't know the outcome of it. After I take you home, if I am taking you home today, I'm meeting Ava at our *haus*. From there, I'm going back to Mildred's *haus* with Ava to see if she might happen to know where Camille's phone is."

"I'd say the police would have it."

"We're hoping they don't."

Elsa-May raised her eyebrows. "I don't want you to be disappointed."

"It wouldn't be the first time. I also want to find out who Camille's friends were. I'm certain Mildred talked about her having a certain friend. Ah, yes, I know where I heard about a friend!"

"Where?"

Ettie took a deep breath while her eyes focused on the ceiling. "It was Kelly. Kelly said that Camille had told a friend of hers that she thought her brother was trying to kill her."

"*Jah*, I remember."

"So, who is this friend and how would we find her? I wonder how well she knew Camille."

"Kelly would have to know who the woman was."

Ettie scratched her head. "*Ach*, there's so much to remember."

"You're having trouble remembering things?"

Ettie glared at her sister and narrowed her eyes. "No more than usual."

Elsa-May chuckled.

Right then, the doctor walked in, followed by two younger men in white coats who, Ettie assumed, were students. The doctor murmured a 'hello' to the two ladies and barely made eye contact. He studied Elsa-May's chart.

He looked at Elsa-May and walked up to stand by her shoulder. "How are you feeling today?"

"Much better today, Doctor. I feel ready to go home."

"Your blood pressure is a little higher than it has been." He examined Elsa-May's leg. "You've got someone to look after you at home?"

"My sister." Elsa-May pointed to Ettie.

The doctor looked at Ettie and gave her a faint smile. Ettie smiled back. The doctor then spoke in low tones to the two men about Elsa-May's chart. He walked to the end of the bed and placed the chart neatly, hooking it over the end of the railing. "I'll sign the discharge papers and a nurse will be here soon to give you instructions for when you're at home."

"Very good, Doctor. Thank you."

When the nurse came and gave Elsa-May her discharge instructions, Ettie called Ava's mother's place to let Ava know that they would soon be leaving the hospital.

"Ettie, I've got something to tell you," Ava said when she got on the phone. "My *mudder* told me something very interesting and I can't wait to tell you."

"What is it?" Ettie asked.

"I'll tell you when I see you."

"What's it about? About Jacob?"

"Kind of."

"About Camille?"

"Ettie, I'll tell you when I see you."

Ettie sighed and then noticed a nurse was glaring at her while waiting for Elsa-May to get into the wheelchair. "We're just about to leave the ward. Then we'll be home as fast as the taxi can take us."

"I'll see you soon," Ava said.

"Can you just give me a little hint?" It was too late – Ava had already hung up.

CHAPTER 14

$\mathcal{T}$he taxi driver helped the sisters into the house. Ettie paid the driver and as soon as he drove off in his car, Ettie looked up, hearing the clip-clop of a horse's hooves.

"Here she is already," Ettie called out to her sister. "Oh, I do hate leaving you after you've just come home."

Elsa-May said, "I'll be all right. Help me into bed and I'll have a little sleep."

Ettie gave Ava a little wave to let her know she wouldn't be long.

Once Ettie got Elsa-May into bed, she walked out of the room and looked at the small bag that Elsa-May had brought back from the hospital with her. Ettie peeped in to see dirty laundry. "That'll have to be done some day, but not today." She picked up the bag and threw it in the laundry room at the back of the house. Before she left, she looked back in at Elsa-May and was pleased to see her eyes closed and her mouth opened. She noticed her chest slowly rising and falling before she gently closed the bedroom door.

Ettie climbed into the buggy to see Ava's excited face. "Well, don't keep *en aldi hutzel* waiting. What did you find out?"

Ava clicked her horse forward into a slow trot. "You won't believe it."

"What?"

"My mother also saw Camille arguing with a woman, a dark-haired woman, at the farmers' markets. And you know why she saw her there?" Ettie shook her head. "Because she was sitting at the same coffee shop nearly next to them."

"Nee!" Ettie shrieked. "Did she hear what they said?"

"Nee, but the thing is, I showed *Mamm* the picture of the doctor, you know, the one we got from my friend who works at the DMV?"

"Was it the same woman?"

"Mamm said she was certain it was the same woman. She remembers because she thought at the time that it was odd to see them together."

"What sort of argument was it? Were there raised voices, that kind of thing?"

"Mamm said they were speaking crossly to each other. From what she said, their voices weren't raised or anything of the kind, but they looked and sounded angry."

"Well, we're finally getting somewhere. The woman she was arguing with was a doctor and now we just have to find out what the two were to each other. Did they know each other as friends or was Camille a patient?" Ettie grabbed Ava's arm. *"Denke, Ava."*

Ava smiled back at Ettie, and then turned her horse down the Eshes' driveway.

"I do hope Crowley's been able to do something helpful," Ettie said. "He didn't say when he'd contact me again."

"Well, he knows where you live. He'll find you when, and if, he's got something to tell you."

Ettie nodded.

Ava stopped the horse and buggy outside Mildred's house.

Ettie rested awhile before getting out of the buggy. She'd planned to visit Mildred to find out who this friend of Camille's was, but wasn't it the police who'd mentioned that Camille had a friend she'd confided in?

"Oh, dear, I think the person I need to speak to next is Detective Kelly."

"Well, we're here now and she's probably seen us."

Ettie nodded. "Let's see how she's holding up. Then do you mind taking me into town to talk to Detective Kelly?"

"*Nee,* I don't mind. I don't have anywhere else I need to be."

"*Denke.*"

"I'll follow your lead. Don't forget we were going to ask about the cell phone," Ava said.

Ettie nodded and then they both walked up to Mildred's *haus* and knocked on the front door. After a while with no answer, they knocked again.

"That's most unusual – she's not answering. She's always looking out when she hears a buggy."

"Shall we check the garden out the back?"

Ettie nodded at Ava's suggestion. Once they were around the back of the house, they walked the length of the garden. Ettie and Ava looked up when they heard a window open. They saw Mildred, with her long gray hair falling around her shoulders, looking as though she'd just woken up. "Ettie, and Ava! I'm so glad you've come. I'll be down in a minute. Let yourselves in." Then she closed the window.

Ettie and Ava smiled at each other. "She's just woken up," Ettie said.

"Seems so."

Ettie and Ava had been sitting in Mildred's living room for over five minutes before Mildred made an appearance. She came walking down the stairs fiddling with her prayer *kapp*.

"Are you feeling okay, Mildred?" Ettie asked.

"I'm okay; just couldn't find a reason to get out of bed."

"Ettie and I have got the water boiling."

"*Denke*. Have you eaten breakfast?" Mildred asked the ladies.

"We have," Ava answered.

"I've been to the hospital already and taken Elsa-May home."

"Oh good. She's better then?"

"She is. She'll just need a little bit of looking after." Ettie made a mental note to go home after their meeting with Mildred and make Elsa-May a meal before they went to see the detective. "Come on, you sit in the kitchen and Ava and I will make you some breakfast."

Mildred nodded and once they reached the kitchen,

she slumped into a chair. "I didn't realize it was so late. I normally get up and cook Jacob breakfast before he starts work. I wonder why he didn't wake me."

"Most likely he wanted you to get some more sleep."

Mildred held her head in her hands. Ettie and Ava looked at each other and Ettie wondered what she could do to make Mildred feel better.

"Would you happen to have Camille's phone here?" Ettie asked.

Mildred was silent for a moment then shook her head. *"Nee.* I think she would've had that at her apartment."

Ettie nodded. She'd known it was a long shot that the phone would be there. After they sat with Mildred for a while, they said goodbye and headed out to Ava's buggy.

"Where to now?" Ava picked up the reins.

"I did want to talk to Kelly, but I think I should go and give Elsa-May some food and see if she needs anything."

After they spent some time with Elsa-May, giving her a meal and talking to her, they left her alone again and headed to see detective Kelly.

"Are you sure you're up to this, Ettie? It's a lot of running around for you."

Ettie gave a little laugh. "I've got no choice. I can't have Jacob going to jail for a crime he didn't do." It was very much on Ettie's mind that Jacob could have a much worse fate than jail, the laws being what they were. Jacob could face the death penalty, in the worst-case scenario. Ettie shook her head as if doing so would shake all the bad images of Jacob being found guilty from her head.

Ettie waited for Ava to park the buggy securely and then they walked up the road to the police station together. As they approached the station, Ettie saw Detective Crowley walking towards them.

"That's Detective Crowley right there," Ettie said to Ava in a low voice.

"I know. I met him. You introduced us when he was helping with Horace's murder investigation."

They stopped still and waited for Detective Crowley.

When he was standing in front of them, Ettie said, "We were just going to come in and tell you, well, tell Detective Kelly, something."

Crowley nodded to the coffee shop two doors up from where they were standing.

"Let's go in there and chat. I've got something to tell you as well."

Once they were seated, Ettie started out by telling Crowley that Ava's mother had said that Dr. Mackelvanner was the one she'd seen arguing with Camille. "Now that we know that, do you think Detective Kelly will look into Camille's medical records?"

"What I think is that Kelly won't see it as having any relevance to the case – not with the evidence that he's got against Jacob."

"Surely he'd have to investigate every avenue to make sure they've got the right person." Ettie ground her teeth in frustration.

"I'll tell you what," Crowley began. "I know someone in the hospital who owes me a favor. I'll have him get me the number of the doctor's private office phone, and I'll speak with her. Then we can go from there. How does that sound?"

"You'd do that? You'd go and talk to the doctor?" Ettie asked.

"Of course I would. I'll call him right now and get the number."

While they waited for their coffee, Crowley made his phone call. A minute later, Crowley was scratching down a phone number on a paper napkin.

"That was easy," Ava said.

Crowley ended his phone conversation and looked up at the two ladies in front of him. "I've got her number. I'll talk to her and then we'll know more."

"That's good of you. Thank you," Ettie said.

Crowley smiled. "How is Elsa-May today?"

"She's fine; we were just there giving her a meal. She's glad to be home."

CHAPTER 15

The next day, Ettie heard a knock on the door and hoped it was Crowley with information.

She opened the door, pleased to see it was indeed Crowley standing there with a smile on his face. She hoped that meant good news. "Do come in."

Ettie stepped aside to let the former detective into her home. He greeted Elsa-May who was lying on the couch propped up by pillows.

"You sit down and talk to Elsa-May. You're just in time for tea; I just boiled the pot."

Ettie had persuaded Elsa-May to lie on the couch instead of staying in her bed. It wasn't long before Ettie was back out in the living room pouring tea for Crowley.

"I'm anxious to know what you've learned from the doctor. Did you speak to her?" Ettie asked while she poured three cups of tea, setting one where Elsa-May could easily reach it.

"I did."

She passed Crowley a cup of tea, waiting for him to continue as she set down her own cup.

"I spoke to the doctor."

He seemed to be hesitating and Ettie wondered if the news was bad.

Ettie couldn't wait. "And what did you find out?"

"Something very interesting; something that I hadn't expected in the least."

The suspense was too much for her and Crowley wasn't helping her trembling hands with the way he was drawing things out. Ettie placed her teacup down on a table. "Go on."

Crowley rubbed his nose and his lips twitched. "Dr. Mackelvanner had been in contact with Mrs Esh, Jacob, and Camille. Nehemiah died in the hospital. Mackelvanner assisted the coroner and she wanted to run further tests but the coroner didn't agree. The coroner put his death down as heart disease, but for weeks something was nagging in the back of Mackelvanner's mind." He looked down into the teacup in his hands and slowly raised it to his lips.

Ettie looked over at Elsa-May, and when their eyes met, Elsa-May raised her eyebrows.

Once he took a sip of tea and the teacup was back on the saucer, he continued. "Her suspicions caused her to go over the coroner's head and go to the police."

"What were her suspicions, Detective?" Elsa-May asked bluntly.

"She feared he might have been poisoned."

Ettie's hand flew to her mouth.

"Then what happened?" Elsa-May asked.

"Her request for the body to be exhumed was denied. The only way to confirm or eliminate her suspicions was to get permission from the family to exhume the body, once the courts denied her request. That's when she contacted Mrs. Esh."

"Mildred did say she thought the doctor's name was familiar. I don't know how she wouldn't remember something as important as that, though," Ettie said. "The doctor really thinks Nehemiah was poisoned?"

"Correct. According to the doctor, Mrs. Esh referred her to the son, and the son didn't want to make the decision unless his sister agreed."

"And she met with Camille and they argued?" Ettie asked.

"She states that she did meet with Camille Esh on two different occasions and Camille was dead against it – pardon the pun. Dr. Mackelvanner said that Jacob agreed to it on the proviso that his sister also agreed. And there's something else I have to tell you."

Ettie took a deep breath. "Go on."

Crowley ran his tongue across the outside of his teeth as if his mouth was dry.

"Have more tea," Elsa-May suggested.

Crowley took a sip of tea, and then said, "It's nothing to be concerned about. I was at the station this morning, before I came here, to tell Kelly what I'd learned about the doctor and her suspicions. I ran into Jacob Esh at the station. I recognized him from the newspaper. I introduced myself to him and told him I was a friend of the both of you. I hope neither of you mind?"

"Not at all," Elsa May said, as Ettie waved a hand to dismiss his concern.

"And what did he say?" Ettie asked.

"I asked if he'd ever had a conversation with the doctor. He told me that the doctor first approached his stepmother and he said Mildred never made any decisions on her own. That's when the doctor spoke to Jacob. Because he never got along with his sister, he was loathe to agree alone that his father's body be touched. He referred the doctor to Camille and gave her Camille's cell phone number. And that's the last he heard from the doctor. Camille never mentioned the doctor to him and he never brought the subject up."

"Camille never mentioned that she'd met with the doctor?" Ettie asked.

"And met with the doctor more than once?" Elsa-May added.

"That's right. He said his sister never mentioned it to him and he never mentioned it to her. He admits to the fact that his sister never got along with him or he with her."

"I wonder why the authorities denied the doctor's request? Especially since the doctor had such suspicions."

"I thought about that and I spoke to a man I know at the courthouse. According to him there has to be 'good cause and exigent circumstances' for a body to be exhumed for an autopsy."

"And what does 'exigent circumstances' mean? I haven't come across that term before," Elsa-May said.

Crowley took a small notebook out of the top pocket of his shirt. "I wrote it down. Let's see now." He flipped some pages over. "Ah, here it is. It means that there must be clear evidence of probable cause."

"So, the doctor didn't have enough evidence to satisfy the court?"

"That's what it sounds like," Crowley said.

"Surely she had enough evidence to raise her suspicions. Wouldn't that have been enough?" Elsa-May asked.

Crowley shook his head. "It seems the court didn't think what evidence she had warranted such action. The state can't go digging up bodies willy-nilly."

"Does Kelly know about the doctor wanting to run more tests on Nehemiah?" Ettie asked.

"I went to tell him, but he wasn't there. He'll be back later today, after two o'clock."

"Under the circumstances, with Camille being murdered, do you think the police might be interested in exhuming the body now?"

Crowley placed his tea on the table in front of him. "It could go two ways. It might make things worse for Jacob if they find his father was poisoned. Have you considered that Kelly might think Jacob killed not only Camille but his father as well?"

Elsa-May shook her head. "I never thought of that."

Ettie glanced at the clock on the wall. "Two hours to go until two."

Crowley said, "Ettie, why don't we visit Mrs. Esh? We can ask her about the doctor."

"I've questioned her about the doctor before."

"Maybe she'll remember something she's forgotten."

CHAPTER 16

rowley and Ettie sat in Mildred's living room. They'd said yes to tea and Mildred was busy in the kitchen preparing it.

"I'll help her. I won't be a moment," Ettie said to Crowley.

"Take your time. I don't know if I can fit another cup in anyway, just yet."

Ettie smiled, and then said, "Sip slowly."

When Ettie entered the kitchen, Mildred said, "He's a friend of yours?"

"*Jah*, he's here to help Jacob. He believes he's innocent, and he just wants to ask you some questions. It'll help Jacob." While Ettie placed cups and saucers on a tray she wondered how she'd feel if someone wanted to dig up her late husband's body. Would she want to know if he'd been poisoned? It wouldn't bring him back.

Mildred poured boiling water into the teapot. "Okay, just a few more minutes and it'll be ready to pour. I'll carry the teapot, Ettie, and you carry the tray."

They placed the tray and the teapot on the low table between the two couches in the living room.

When Mildred sat down, she said, "You said you wanted to talk to me about a doctor?"

"That's right. Do you remember speaking to a doctor who wanted to exhume Nehemiah's body to run some tests?" Crowley asked. "Her name is Dr. Mackelvanner."

Mildred glanced at Ettie, and then looked back at the detective. "Ettie mentioned that name to me. I remember now that I did speak to her. She said she wanted to run some further tests but I said it was too late; he was buried. She wouldn't take no for an answer and kept talking at me. Eventually I told her to speak to Jacob since he's the man of the house now and probably should make all the decisions." She fiddled with the strings of her prayer *kapp*. "Why is it so important?"

"It seems the doctor has reason to believe your husband might have been murdered. And this doctor was seen arguing with your daughter on at least one, and possibly two, occasions," Crowley said.

"You mean stepdaughter," Mildred corrected him sternly.

Ettie was a little surprised; she'd never heard Mildred correct anybody from saying 'daughter' to 'stepdaughter'. She'd always called Jacob her son, so it seemed a little odd since she'd insisted recently that she treated them both the same.

"Yes, I'm sorry, stepdaughter," Crowley corrected himself.

"I'm not surprised that the doctor was arguing with Camille. Camille could send anyone crazy. You could be in a good mood and then Camille would say something hateful. She was like that. I think she liked to make people unhappy. If I didn't know any better I'd think she was the child of the devil."

Ettie nearly choked on the tea she was about to swallow. She coughed. Crowley put his tea down and patted Ettie on the back. Ettie coughed again.

"Oh dear, do you want some water?" Mildred asked.

"*Jah,*" Ettie managed to say.

When Mildred was out of the room Ettie looked at Crowley.

"She's full of hate for an Amish person," Crowley said.

"I've never heard her say anything like that before," Ettie whispered.

Mildred hurried back. "There you go, Ettie."

Ettie took a mouthful of water. "Ah, that's better. *Denke.*"

"About that doctor. I don't know why she wanted to do more tests. I didn't listen to what she had to say properly, but Nehemiah was dead and that was that. Jacob must have felt the same."

"You didn't talk to him about it?" Crowley asked. "The doctor told me that Jacob agreed, but only if his sister agreed as well."

"No. I gave him the number to call the doctor and then after he called her we never spoke of it again. He didn't tell me what he said to her and I never asked." Mildred crinkled her nose. "Everybody was scared of her and her anger; it just wasn't right."

"The doctor?" Ettie asked.

Mildred shook her head. "Camille. She was so full of

bitterness and hatred toward Jacob she didn't want to – just didn't want him to have any little bit of happiness in his life. I suppose he was too scared to say 'yes' to the doctor and face Camille's anger if she'd disagreed."

Ettie nodded. "Didn't the doctor go into details when she was speaking to you of why she wanted Nehemiah's body exhumed?"

"I wasn't really listening. She said something about her not being happy with some test that she'd run and then I didn't really want to hear any more."

Crowley said, "She thinks she found evidence in the body of poisoning consistent with a substance called ethylene glycol, a common coolant used in motor vehicles."

Ettie gasped. "That's one of the poisons also found in Camille's body," Ettie said. "I didn't know that's what the doctor had found."

Crowley rubbed his jaw. "I guess I should have said so, but I didn't know that's what Camille died from."

"I thought I told you," Ettie said. "They found that poison and also another poison, which was sleeping tablets or something of the sort."

"They found that ethy... whatever it was in the barn. Jacob and I thought that Nehemiah must've used it to protect his metal tools."

Ettie rubbed her head. She jumped when she heard a loud bashing sound on Mildred's door. Seeing Mildred look so worried, Crowley jumped to his feet. "Shall I get that?"

Mildred nodded and then Ettie and Mildred followed

Crowley, staying back a little way. Ettie wondered whether it was the police.

When Crowley opened the door, Ettie saw a red-faced Mr. Bradshaw from next door. "Where's Mrs. Esh?" he demanded.

"She's here. What's this about?"

"Who are you?"

"A friend of the family." Crowley put one arm up on the doorframe.

The man looked into the house. "Where is she?"

Crowley turned around to look at Mildred, and then Mildred stepped forward so Bradshaw could see her. "Yes?"

"I've just had the police come round and tell me that my fingerprints were found on the coolant you had in your barn. I told them, and now I'll tell you. I had that tin in my shed and you or your son stole it. That's why my fingerprints would've been on it. I'm not guilty of killing anyone." He stopped to take a breath. "Now, one of you stole it off my property and then killed someone with it. I want you or your son to admit to stealing it. I'm not going to prison for something I didn't do."

"Calm down. I'm sure the police just wanted to talk to you," Crowley said.

"What would you know? They said I should get a lawyer and they'll be speaking to me again."

Crowley took a step toward the man. "I think you should leave. Mrs. Esh has been through enough. Sounds like the police aren't accusing you of anything."

"Not yet they aren't." He took a step back and pointed

his finger at Mildred. "Just get your coward son to admit to stealing it." He turned and strode away.

Ettie put her arm around Mildred's shoulder and felt her shaking. "Come, Mildred, sit back down," Ettie said and then steered her back to the living room.

"I'm sorry," Crowley said, following the two women. "I should've told him you weren't home."

"No. He might have come back when I was by myself."

Ettie sat next to Mildred. "Well, that explains what the poison was doing in the barn."

"No it doesn't; not really, because we still don't know who put it there," Crowley said, slumping into the couch.

"Does that mean that Jacob's prints weren't on the tin of poison?" Ettie asked.

"I'll find out." Crowley whipped his cell phone out of his pocket and walked outside.

Ettie turned to Mildred. "See? Things are looking good. If Jacob's prints weren't on the tin, then that should help his case."

Mildred swallowed hard and nodded.

When Crowley came back inside, he said, "They found two sets of prints: Bradshaw's, and... I'm afraid they found yours, Mildred."

Ettie looked at Mildred.

"I never go into the barn. How would my prints have gotten onto the thing? I hope they don't think I killed Nehemiah or Camille."

"When was the last time you went to the barn?"

"Maybe, um... I do recall I went in there a few weeks ago to fetch a stronger broom. The house broom was too soft to get some dirt off the back steps."

"The good thing is that Jacob's prints weren't found," Ettie said.

Crowley frowned. "We're going to need more than that to get him off."

Ettie and Ava stayed with Mildred until Jacob came home. When Crowley was driving Ettie home he said, "Are you still going through that list of names and addresses that Kelly gave you?"

"I am. Well, Ava is."

"Keep working through the list; there must be a clue in there somewhere. There's something we're missing."

"Will do. And while I'm doing that, can you see what else Kelly has found out?"

"I'll visit him tomorrow and come to your place in the afternoon."

CHAPTER 17

*T*he next morning, Ettie got herself ready to go and see Ava Glick. She hoped Ava would have a free day to help her work through that phone list. Leah Miller kept coming to mind. She was someone who they could visit and she might know what was going on with Camille in those last weeks of her life.

When the taxi drew close to Ava's place, Ettie could see the horse in the paddock and she knew that Ava would be home. Ettie knocked on her door and waited. Ava opened the door. "Ettie!"

"Hello. I was hoping we could go over the phone list of Camille's again."

"I have to help my *mudder* today at the market."

Ettie nodded.

"Tell you what. I'll go there and see if she really needs me. She might not mind if I help her tomorrow instead."

"That would be good."

After they hitched the wagon, they traveled to the farmers' markets and Ettie told Ava all that had happened.

"So I was thinking we should go and pay Leah Miller a visit."

"That's if it's the same Leah Miller that we know. There could be a lot of people with that name."

"*Nee,* it has to be the same one. She looked exactly the same in her photograph, only a little older."

"Yes, she did. Well, that will be our first call, if I don't have to work."

"I'll come in with you and talk to your *mudder*. I'll tell her I want to borrow you for the day."

Ava giggled. "Okay."

Their plan worked. Ava was able to have the day off if she worked the next day instead.

Once they were in the buggy again, Ava said, "You do have a way of talking people into things, Ettie."

"Do I? Now, where's that list?"

Ava pulled the list out from behind her seat and handed it to Ettie.

"Leah doesn't live far, but let's take your horse back and go by taxi. We'll cover more ground."

Ava turned the horse around and Ettie called a taxi from the shanty down the road.

ETTIE HAD the taxi wait for them while they knocked on the door of the address that was given to them. There were three small villa-apartments attached to one another. Leah's, according to their list, was number two. Ettie knocked on the door and her heart pounded heavily. What would she say to Leah? Leah hadn't gone to

Camille's funeral, so had they been friends at all? Perhaps not.

"She's not home," someone yelled from the next-door property.

Ettie and Ava looked over the fence to see a young man.

"Do you know where she is?" Ava asked.

"At work, I'd say."

"Does she work close by?"

"Down at the ice-creamery."

"Sprinkles?"

"Yeah, that's the one," the young man said.

"Thank you," Ettie said.

"No problem."

As they were walking back to the taxi, Ettie asked Ava, "You know where that is?"

Ava nodded. *"Jah.* I love ice cream and they have the best in town."

"What name does Leah go by now?"

"Lacey Miller."

"That's right."

This time when the taxi pulled up at the ice-creamery, they paid the driver and let him go. "If she's not here we can have some ice cream. I won't be having ice cream for quite a while now that Elsa-May has to cut down on her food."

"You can't eat less, Ettie; you're already thin."

"I always stay the same weight no matter how much or how little I eat. I've got a good constitution. Elsa-May was always on the heavy side. I can't eat ice cream in front of her."

Ava giggled. "I suppose not. That would be cruel."

The building they were walking toward was just at the town's edge. It was a white double-story building with white tables and chairs outside, and a pink and white umbrella over every table.

"Shall we sit inside or out?" Ettie asked.

"Maybe we should sit inside. There might be more chance of seeing Leah."

"Okay, you go first."

Ava walked in through the automatic-opening glass sliding door, and Ettie followed. Ettie scanned the faces of the girls behind the counter and couldn't see Leah. They looked at the array of ice creams, sorbets, and gelatos. Ava ordered a strawberry delight, which was a scoop each of strawberry sorbet and strawberry ice cream topped with cream and strawberry slivers, all sprinkled with dark chocolate flakes.

Ettie ordered a coffee-choc surprise, which had coffee and chocolate ice cream, dark Dutch chocolate ice cream, and whipped cream with white chocolate slivers.

They were given numbers for their orders and told to take a seat.

When Ava was given her number she asked, "Is Lacey working today?"

"She's on a break. She'll be back in a minute."

"Oh, good."

Ettie and Ava found a table at the side of the room. There weren't many people sitting inside because it was such a nice day. While they waited, Ava produced the list of names. She pointed to a man's name. "We should look at this man next. He's the one who had the criminal record. That is, if it's the same man I read about in the paper."

"A petty criminal. I wonder what Camille was doing talking to him."

"A boyfriend perhaps? People who go on those dating websites meet all kinds of people. They could've gone on a date."

"What are you talking about a dating website for? Was Camille doing that kind of thing?"

Ava shrugged. "Could've been."

They both looked up to see Leah walking toward them carrying their ice creams. Leah had a huge smile and seemed pleased to see them. She greeted them and placed their ice creams down on the table.

Ettie and Ava stood up and hugged her.

"Can you sit with us for a while?" Ettie asked.

Leah nodded. "I'm the manager so I can basically do what I want," she said with a little laugh. "How did you know I worked here? One of the girls said you asked for me."

"We heard you worked here," Ava said. "I've been here before, but I've never seen you here."

"I've not been here long, around three months. I was managing another store in town."

Ettie needed to change the subject so she wouldn't have to tell her she was on Camille's illegally-gotten phone list. Looking at her ice cream, she said, "I don't think I'll be able to get through this. It's huge."

Leah giggled. "What's been happening in the community? I heard about Jacob Esh," she said.

"That's actually what we came to talk to you about," Ava said.

"Yes, were you friends with Camille?"

"Not good friends. We knew each other." Leah breathed out heavily. "I've been bothered by something. I've even had nightmares about it, I feel so guilty. I didn't want to get into trouble so I kept quiet about it, but now seeing you two has made me feel even more guilty about it."

"What is it?" Ettie asked.

Leah leaned forward. "Camille asked me to go to the police and tell them that she thought her brother was trying to kill her."

"So it was you who told the police that?"

Leah nodded. "You heard?"

Ettie nodded. "That's the main reason the police were looking at Jacob."

"Oh no! She said it was just a prank she was playing on her brother."

"What made you do it? It doesn't sound like a prank to me," Ava said.

Leah blinked a couple times and looked away. "She gave me two thousand dollars to do it and I needed the money at the time. I changed my mind after she left, but I did need the money, so I went through with it. She told me exactly what to tell them and she wrote down the date she wanted me to go and see them."

"Do you still have that note?"

"I wouldn't think so. I don't keep anything I don't need. When I found out she'd been killed I felt really bad about going to the police, but if he's innocent he'll have nothing to worry about."

"Do you think that Camille did think her brother was trying to kill her?" Ava asked.

She shrugged. "I don't know. I felt awful when I found out what happened to Camille, and then that they'd arrested Jacob. They came around and I had to go back to the station and verify what I'd told them. I didn't tell them that she asked me - and paid me - to say it. I lied to them. I've been so worried; I don't want to get into trouble by telling them I lied to them twice. The first time I went there I didn't even know that Camille had already died."

"You must tell them, Leah," Ava said.

"Lacey. It's Lacey now," Leah said.

"Sorry, Lacey. They're heavily relying on that information and it's making Jacob look guilty. Now with everything else they're finding out, they're framing it in the reference that he was trying to kill her, if you see what I mean." Ava's voice trailed away.

Leah breathed out heavily. "Could I get charged or something?"

Ettie patted Leah's hand. "I don't think you'll get into trouble. They just want to know the truth."

Ava added, "It's possible Jacob might be charged with murder if they find him guilty."

Leah's eyes opened wide. "I'll go to the police when I finish work."

"Could you do it now?" Ettie asked.

"We'll go with you," Ava said.

"Would you?"

Ettie and Ava nodded.

"I'll take the rest of the day off, then. You wait here and I'll get my things."

When Leah left them, Ettie and Ava looked down at their ice creams.

"I'll race you," Ava said.

"*Nee*, ice cream should be eaten slowly and savored." Ettie pushed her spoon into the coffee flavored ice cream as that was her favorite flavor. She could smell the strong coffee aroma before she placed it into her mouth. The texture was smooth and creamy.

Ava had pushed the cream and the strawberries aside and was spooning the strawberry ice cream into her mouth as quickly as she could.

"We must come back here another day," Ettie said as she loaded her spoon with both coffee and chocolate ice cream.

Ava's mouth was full so she could only nod.

Leah sat down again. She had her bag over one shoulder, a sweater over one arm, and a car key in her hand hanging from a keychain.

"You've got a car?" Ettie asked.

"Yes. I'll drive us there. Don't hurry; I'll wait until you finish."

"No. I think we're ready. Aren't we, Ettie?"

"I'm good to go."

Leah led the way out to a small Honda Civic. It was only a two-door, so Ava squeezed past the front seat into the back, and Ettie sat in the front.

"I'm so glad you both came in today. This was

weighing heavily on me. I'll feel so much better once I tell the truth."

"The truth sets us free," Ettie said.

"I'll have to pay back the money she gave me. I don't have it right now, but I must go and see Mrs. Esh to tell her I'll pay it back."

"Who were you speaking to at the station?" Ettie asked.

"He was a detective. I don't remember his name."

"What did he look like?"

"Hard to describe. He just looked like a detective, I guess."

"Detective Kelly's the one looking into things."

"Yes, that's it. I'm sure that was his name."

Ettie was satisfied that the police would have one less piece of evidence against Jacob. Without Leah's testimony there was no proof that Camille had feared for her life from Jacob. Now it would be known that Camille had said she was playing a prank – little did Camille know that she'd be dead when the prank played out.

CHAPTER 18

After Leah Miller made her confession to Detective Kelly about taking part in Camille's prank, Kelly wasn't at all happy and Leah was in tears. When Leah came out of his office, she told Ettie and Ava between sobs that Kelly had warned her in a nasty manner of the seriousness of what she'd done.

"Are you all right to drive, Leah?" Ava asked when the three women were standing together on the front steps of the police station.

Leah wiped her nose with a tissue. "I'm okay. Can I drive you two home?"

Ava and Ettie looked at each other, and then Ettie said, "Ava and I have some things to do in town. Thank you once again for being honest. It will help Jacob out of the mess he's in."

"Good. I can't imagine he'd do a thing like that."

Ava asked, "You wouldn't happen to know a man called Nick Heaton, would you?"

Leah thought for a moment. "No. I don't recall that I do. Why?"

"He was someone Camille knew. I was just wondering if you knew him too."

After Leah left, Ava said, "I wonder if Kelly has found out any more about the people on the list? Especially because Nick Heaton might have a criminal record if, he's the same one I found on the Internet."

"Shall we go in and ask? By the sound of things he's not in a good mood."

Just then Kelly came out of the building.

"Mrs. Smith and her side-kick."

Ava screwed up her nose.

"We were just coming in to speak to you."

"I know you think things are looking better for Jacob Esh, but we've just found out something to make our case even stronger."

"You have?"

"The will that Camille conveniently wrote just days before she died was written by Jacob."

"No. That's not possible."

"It's possible, it's probable, and it happened. We have a forensic handwriting analyst who's willing to testify that the will was not written by the hand of Camille Esh, and that it was, in fact, written by the hand of her brother, Jacob Esh."

"Jacob's fingerprints weren't found on the tin of the poison that killed her."

"He could well have used gloves."

"What about the man next door? His fingerprints were found and he wanted the farm. With Camille killed and

Jacob in jail for murder, Mildred would most likely sell the farm."

"We talked to him. He claims the tin was stolen from him and that's why his prints were on it."

"And you believed him? Why don't you believe Jacob? If he shot at her while she was in her apartment, why was the gun just left with all his other guns? Wouldn't he have hidden the gun somewhere?"

"Perhaps he wasn't aware that the gun could be traced. He is Amish, after all, and like all you people he's only had a limited education."

"If you knew anything about us you'd know that some of us continue our schooling from home." Ava said bluntly, "And Jacob lived outside the Amish community for about twenty years."

Ettie could see Ava was getting upset so she put her hand on Ava's arm. "Let's go, Ava."

Ettie and Ava went home in separate taxis. Feeling completely defeated, Ettie pushed the front door open. She was pleased to see Elsa-May sitting up and looking brighter.

"I'm sorry I've hardly been here today."

"You look dreadful."

"I'll put the dinner on and then I'll sit with you and tell you all about it. Things aren't looking good for Jacob."

An hour later, Ettie had told Elsa-May all that had happened that day.

"They can tell that Camille didn't write the will?"

"Apparently so."

"It is beginning to look like he's guilty. It doesn't make

sense that she would get Leah to tell the police she thought Jacob was trying to kill her."

"Perhaps she was acting out of spite since he got the farm. She might have been trying to disrupt his life by having the police come and question him, or something like that."

A knock sounded on their door.

"That might be Ava. She was very upset by what Kelly said to us. He was really quite rude when speaking about our community and the people in it."

Ettie swung the door open to see old Detective Crowley. "When are you ladies going to get a phone?"

"Crowley! Come in."

The former detective walked in and sat down. "How are you, Elsa-May?"

"I'm so much better. I feel better than I've felt in a long time."

Ettie sat down on the couch. "Do you have news?"

Crowley gave a sharp nod. "I do. I struggled with myself for a while. I know medical records are confidential and I don't have the authority anymore to look into things…"

"Yes?" Elsa-May said.

"I got my friend at the hospital to look up Camille Esh's file. Or, in fact, to see if she had a file. Both my contact at the hospital and I could get into a lot of trouble over this, so I have to be careful how I let Kelly know about it."

Ettie was now on the edge of the couch. "About what?"

"Camille had recently been diagnosed with the same fatal disease that you told me her mother died from."

"Oh my," Ettie said. "That's no good."

"And that's how she knew Dr. Mackelvanner?" Elsa-May asked.

Crowley shook his head. "No. She was under a different doctor."

"I haven't told you yet, but we found the woman who told the police that Camille feared Jacob was going to kill her. Camille had paid her to say that. We happened to know the young woman and we went with her to the police station. Kelly wasn't happy about it. She's going to look and see if she's still got the instructions Camille wrote down for her."

"That's one good thing for Jacob," Crowley said. "I'm thinking more that the stepmother, Mildred, might have had some involvement. If Camille told her that she had the disease, might Mildred have killed her to lessen her suffering? I saw Kelly earlier, and he said that Camille's will was a forgery. What if Mildred wanted Jacob to inherit the money Camille had – keep Camille's money with Jacob? Since Camille didn't get along with anyone in her family, she might have preferred her money end up elsewhere."

Ettie pulled her mouth to one side. "I don't think that Mildred is so focused on money, though, Detective. Besides, Kelly said their expert said Jacob wrote the will."

Elsa-May said, "My pick is the neighbor. He seems to have a bad temper and his prints were on the tin of poison. Also, it wouldn't have been hard for him to take the gun, drive past Camille's apartment, shoot at her, and then put the gun back in the house once Mildred had gone out."

"If that's true, the neighbor is taking a very indirect route to get the farm, don't you think? I mean, how could he have thought it all up?" Crowley asked.

"From what Ettie said, Bradshaw didn't like Camille anyway. It seems a good way to solve two problems at once; get rid of the two people who were standing in his way of buying the farm."

Ettie gasped. "It's just occurred to me. Elsa-May could be right. What if Nehemiah was killed by Bradshaw?"

"It could be possible, as they were neighbors and if they met often for a drink in the afternoon or something like that. I think the poison has to be administered over a time," Crowley said.

Ettie shook her head. "I don't think he'd drink or eat with an *Englischer*."

"But we don't know that for certain, Ettie. He probably didn't, but he could've."

"What are you going to do?" Ettie asked Crowley. "Are you going to tell Kelly what you found out about Camille being ill?"

Crowley nodded. "I will, but I'll have to figure out how to do it without appearing to have bent the rules."

"What would you do now, if you were working the case?" Ettie asked.

"I'd have Nehemiah's body exhumed and retested."

Elsa-May said. "Who do you think might have killed him?"

Crowley raised his hands in the air. "We'd have to establish whether he was killed first. No good putting the cart before the horse."

"What else would you do?" Ettie asked.

"Then I'd go through all of Camille's phone contacts and I'd get a second opinion on the handwriting of the will. I'd also get the tin re-examined for further prints. Then I'd talk to Camille's doctor to see if he could shed light on anything."

"Then that's what you must get Kelly to do," Elsa-May said.

Crowley tilted his head and sniffed the air. "That smells delicious."

"Ah. I must turn off the stove." Ettie pushed herself to her feet. "Care to join us for dinner? I've made a pot pie."

"I'd be delighted."

EARLY THE NEXT MORNING, Ava knocked on Ettie and Elsa-May's door. When she was sitting in their living room she said why she'd come.

"I was so upset last night I couldn't settle. So I went to Nick Heaton's."

Ettie's jaw dropped. "Why? Why would you do that?"

"Don't get mad at me; he wasn't there. The man he lived with said he's in jail. We got talking, and I asked him about Camille and he didn't know if his friend knew Camille or anything."

"So it was a wasted trip and you put yourself in danger."

"*Nee*. I haven't finished."

"Go on."

"He remembers one night Nick came home and told him about some lady paying him to have him shoot into an apartment. She gave him gloves to wear, the gun she wanted him to use, and the bullets. Then she'd told him to cover the gun with a towel and leave it in the trash can at a nearby park."

Ettie gasped, "Did you hear that Elsa-May?" she yelled out to Elsa-May, who was still in bed.

"*Jah!* That's interesting, but Kelly won't believe it unless it comes from the man himself. And only Kelly can talk to him if he's in jail," Elsa-May yelled back.

Ava said, "I wanted to come and tell you last night, but I thought you could do with a good night's sleep."

"Crowley visited us last night. He told us that Camille had the same disease that her mother died from."

"That's awful. Is that why she wasn't nice to people? Doesn't it affect the brain or something?"

"It does." Ettie nodded. "Don't tell anyone that Crowley found that out; he did it by illegal means and he has to figure out a way to let Kelly know that Camille was sick. He'll have to find a way to suggest that Kelly look into Camille's medical history."

"From what we know, Camille paid someone to shoot into her apartment and then paid Leah to tell the police she feared for her life."

Ettie shook her head. "What if it was Mildred?"

"Ettie! Isn't she a good friend of yours?"

"*Ach.* I don't know what to think anymore. The more I think about it, the more I find reasons that any number of people could've killed her. Crowley said he's going to see Kelly today and he'll try to push him to do some things."

"That's good. Like what?"

"See Camille's doctor, for one. Then take a second look

for more prints on the bottle of coolant, and get another handwriting expert to take a look at the will for a second opinion. I think that's all. That's all I can remember, anyway."

"That'll be good. It's good to have him on Jacob's side. Have you spoken to Jacob lately?"

"*Nee*. Not for a while, but I think I should. I just can't shake the disappointment about finding out Camille's will was written by him."

"It wouldn't hurt for us to go and visit his *haus* just in time for the midday meal, would it? We know he comes home to eat."

Ettie nodded. "I'll go fix Elsa-May something to eat before we go. Then I must come home and wait for Crowley. He's going to tell me how he got on with Kelly."

CHAPTER 19

*E*ttie and Ava came across Jacob before they reached Mildred's house. He was fixing some fences by the road.

He looked up and waved when he heard them approach. When Ava stopped the buggy, he walked over. "I want to thank you both for helping me. *Mamm* says you've been doing a lot of looking into things."

"We have," Ettie said, climbing down from the buggy. "I do have a question to ask you."

"Sure."

"The detective says that they found out that the will was written in your handwriting."

"Yes, it was."

Ettie frowned at him. "You wrote it yourself?"

He nodded. "Camille came to me and told me that she wanted to write a will and leave the money she had to me. I was shocked, but we were *bruder* and *schweschder* and she had no one else. She met me in the fields, just like how you came across me today, and she had a paper and a pen. She wanted me to write it out because she never had much schooling and wasn't good at writing. I wrote word for word what she asked me to write and then she signed it. She asked me to keep it secret and I never told anyone. I know the police are trying to make something of it."

Ettie shook her head. "It does sound bad."

"It makes sense the way you explain it," Ava said.

Ettie nodded. "I see how it came about."

"Anything else you want to ask me?"

Ettie shook her head. "I can't think of anything for the moment."

"Do you know a man called Nick Heaton?" Ava asked.

"I believe I looked at a used car being sold at one of his car lots. And he might be the man Camille bought her car from."

"One of his car lots?"

"*Jah*, he buys and sells used cars. I think he's got two or three places he sells used cars from."

"Would it surprise you that he's in prison?"

Jacob tipped his hat back on his head. "I suppose it does. What did he do?"

Ava and Ettie looked at each other. Ettie said, "We're not sure yet."

"Well, then I'll have someone I know in there."

"Jacob, you mustn't let those thoughts come into your head."

"I think it's best to be prepared. If I'm found innocent, well and good, and if not, I'll be prepared to face whatever they throw at me. I'm not going to live in fear."

Ettie nodded.

After they said goodbye to Jacob, Ava asked, "Do you want to visit Mildred?"

"Nee, not today. There are some loose ends that I wish Kelly would help us with. Someone should talk to Nick Heaton in prison and see what his dealings were with Camille. The detective talked about looking into the trust fund to see if there was money missing and I never heard any more about it."

"Most likely there was no money missing and Kelly would've put it down to the fact that Jacob knew Camille was leaving him the money anyway."

"Hmm. I wonder if Jacob's told Kelly yet that Camille had him write the will."

"'Says he.' That's what Kelly would say."

Ettie peered into Ava's face. "You're most likely right. Don't you have to work today? Or was it yesterday?"

Ava giggled. *"Mamm* gave me the week off. She could tell my mind was elsewhere and she said they've been quiet."

"Good. Now, I must go home and wait for Crowley. Care to join me?"

Ava nodded. "Let's go."

THAT AFTERNOON, Crowley walked into the house and took a seat.

"How did things go with Kelly?"

"He's put a request to the court to have Nehemiah's body exhumed."

Ettie put her fingers to her mouth. "From what you

said before, I don't know if that's a good thing or a bad thing." Ettie told Crowley how Jacob said it came about that he wrote his sister's will out and she made him say he wouldn't mention it to anyone.

"There's an awful lot against him with only his say-so to defend himself. I know you've never been wrong before, Ettie, but are you really certain this time?"

"I believe in his innocence."

Crowley nodded. "We have to wait and see what Nehemiah's autopsy brings."

"There is the matter of the other people on Camille's phone list. Ava and I found that... Well, I'll let Ava tell you."

Ava told Crowley about what she'd learned from Nick Heaton's flat mate.

"I'm sure Kelly wouldn't mind if I talk to the fellow."

"Really? That would be wonderful."

It was a week later that Crowley came to tell Elsa-May and Ettie that Nehemiah's body was exhumed and re-examined and it was found that Nehemiah's death was not due to poisoning with ethylene glycol.

"Where does that leave Jacob?" Elsa-May asked.

"Have you spoken to that man in prison yet?" Ettie asked.

"Firstly, Elsa-May, I'm not sure where that leaves Jacob. And Ettie, I have spoken to Nick Heaton. We've only just gotten the information out of him. He said he'd only give me information if the courts lessened his sentence."

"What did he say?" Ettie asked.

"The courts cooperated and cut his time in prison down in exchange for him providing information. It was actually Kelly who spoke to him and got his statement."

"And?" Elsa-May asked.

"He said that some woman paid him to shoot a gun into an apartment and when he was done he had to wrap the gun in a towel and leave it in the park."

"That's exactly what his flatmate told Ava."

"He positively identified the woman as Camille Esh."

"From a photograph?" Ettie asked.

"It would have to be from a photograph, Ettie, since the woman's dead."

Ettie pressed her lips together as she stared at her sister.

Crowley added. "He got paid two thousand dollars."

"That must have been her number for everything. It was also the amount that she paid Leah Miller," Ettie said.

"Is Jacob in the clear now?"

"No. Jacob's prints were on the cup in her apartment identified as having poison in it, and Jacob forged the will."

"Yes, but Camille signed the will. Jacob told us how it all happened."

Ettie closed her eyes for a second and then glanced up at the clock on the wall.

"It's four o'clock. Would Kelly still be at the station?"

"I guess so. He probably will be there until seven tonight."

"Will you drive me to see him? I've just figured the whole thing out."

"You have?" Crowley jumped to his feet.

"I'm coming too," Elsa-May said.

"Are you well enough?" Ettie asked.

"I'm not going to miss this."

"I'll call him and tell him we're coming."

CHAPTER 20

*W*hen the four of them were settled in Detective Kelly's office, Kelly leaned back in his chair. "This will be entertaining. Go ahead, Mrs. Smith."

"We have a young girl, Camille Esh. Her mother got sick and was prone to fits of rage. She beat her young daughter, leaving internal scars that would never heal. When Mary died, Camille's father did the best he could for her and her brother. He married another woman, but Camille, even though she was young, never let herself love again."

Detective Kelly laughed. "I didn't know you were a psychiatrist, Mrs. Smith."

Ettie ignored his jab and continued, "The pain of loving and trusting someone only to be betrayed as her mother had betrayed her would be too much. Camille built invisible walls around her heart to save herself from further pain."

"Is this going to take long?" Kelly glanced at his watch.

Ettie cleared her throat, and then said, "Her inner hate of her brother was most likely spurred by the hatred she was shown by her mother. The trauma of her youth never left her. When she found she had inherited the disease her mother had, she hatched a plan. She didn't want to suffer like her mother had and die a death full of mental torture. She decided to end her life, and at the same time, she'd implicate her brother and ruin his life."

"Yes, if she had to go she'd take him with her," Elsa-May added. "Because her father, the only person she loved, had showed preference to her brother by leaving him the farm. She must've been outraged beyond belief.

"That's why she met him in the fields and had him write the will, and she signed it in front of him. He was surprised but she told him not to tell anyone. She took cups from the house after Jacob had used them, and used those same cups at her own apartment."

"So," Kelly said, "she paid Nick Heaton to shoot into her apartment and her other friend to say she thought her brother was trying to kill her. Yes, I must say I did have the same thoughts as you when I heard she had a fatal illness. I even talked to her doctor and found she had asked about the possibility of euthanasia."

"She did?"

"Yes, when she first got the diagnosis," Kelly said nodding. "I had it set in my mind that she killed herself and wanted her brother to take the blame. It's just what a spiteful woman would do and I've known a few of those in my time, believe me. She found out she didn't have long to live, so she poisons herself with the coolant, doesn't like how painful it is, so she speeds things along with a dose of pills, grinds them down into a drink and drinks them in a cup with Jacob's fingerprints that she's gotten from her stepmother's house. She dies and no one knows about her illness or the fact that she's paid people to bolster up her evil plot with evidence against her older brother."

"So you believe me?" Ettie asked.

"Like I said, I had come to the same conclusion as you, until I had the forensic team have another look at that signature on Camille Esh's will."

"And?" Crowley asked.

"We got a sample of handwriting from Mrs. Esh, and I'm afraid it's a match."

"A match to Mildred's handwriting?"

"That's right, Mrs. Smith. The signature on the will was in the handwriting of Mildred Esh. The body of the text was in Jacob's handwriting as he admits, but he was lying about Camille signing it."

A hush fell across the room.

Detective Kelly turned to Ettie. "You don't know who you can trust, Mrs. Smith. I believe I told you days ago that sometimes people can do things that surprise even themselves." He glanced at his watch. "It's too late now, but tomorrow I'm going to have Mildred Esh explain herself to me."

"You haven't spoken with her yet?" Crowley asked.

"The handwriting report only just came through." Kelly looked at Ettie. "I was beginning to listen to you and look for other possibilities, but now I know Jacob has been lying about the will. What else has he been lying about?"

Ettie didn't say anything, remembering that Mildred's prints had been found on the bottle of ethylene glycol. Could Mildred have had something to do with Camille's death?

On the way out of the station, Ettie said to Crowley, "What's the time now?"

He looked at his watch. "A little before five."

"Feel like a visit to Mildred?" Ettie whispered.

"Kelly is intending on talking to her tomorrow," Elsa-May said.

"Exactly why we should go now," Ettie said

Crowley nodded and drove the ladies to Mildred's house. Before they pulled up, Ettie said, "Let me do the talking."

"I was intending to," Crowley said. "Because I've got no idea what you're up to."

Once they were seated in Mildred's house, Ettie asked, "What time do you expect Jacob home?"

"In another hour or so."

"Mildred, I'm afraid I've got something to tell you," Ettie said.

Mildred raised her eyebrows.

"Detective Kelly is coming here tomorrow to ask you to go into the station for questioning."

"About what?"

"I think you know." Ettie stared at Mildred until Mildred looked away.

Then Mildred put her head in her hands. "I thought it was a harmless thing to do."

"What was?" Crowley asked and then he got a sharp dig in the ribs from Ettie's elbow.

"Go on. You'll feel better if you tell us," Ettie said.

Mildred looked up at them and they saw her eyes brimming with tears. "I didn't think there would be any harm. I mean, the money would most likely have gone to Jacob anyway. Camille didn't write the will, but I heard the government takes out a lot of money if someone hasn't left a will. I don't know if that's true, but that's what I've heard."

"So you and Jacob wrote that will and not Camille?" Ettie asked.

Jacob stepped into the room. "That's right."

All heads turned to look at Jacob as he loomed in the doorway of the living room. He took a few more steps into the room and sat down next to his stepmother. "I'm sorry I lied about that, but I was just trying to protect my *mudder.*"

"It was my idea, not Jacob's. The money had come from Nehemiah and he would've wanted it to go to Jacob. I forced Jacob to do it."

"Did you also make Jacob end Camille's life to prevent her suffering?" Crowley asked.

"No! We'd never do anything like that. I don't know who killed her. It wasn't me or my mother." Jacob placed his arm around his stepmother.

Ettie turned and looked at Crowley before she licked her lips and added, "Remember what Kelly said? He thought what I thought, except when he found out about the will."

A loud knock sounded on the door, causing Ettie to jump.

Jacob sprang to his feet to answer it. Loud voices were heard, and a few seconds later Kelly walked into the room.

"And here we all are," Kelly said, looking at each person in turn. "When I saw you all hurrying away from the station, I guessed this would be the place you were heading."

"Have a seat, Detective," Jacob said. "I may as well tell you what it was I just told them."

Kelly sat down in the only spare armchair. "Go ahead."

"My mother and I are responsible for writing that will. The will was the only thing I lied about to you, and for that, I'm sorry."

"So you admit to falsifying a legal document?"

"Yes," Jacob nodded.

"That's a serious crime. It's a felony in the third degree. You could both face jail time and a hefty fine."

Mildred leaned forward. "It was my idea, and I was the one who signed it, so I'm just as guilty as Jacob. No, I'm more guilty because it was all my idea."

Detective Kelly shook his head. "This is interesting. Mrs. Esh, you admit to forging your stepdaughter's will and your fingerprints are on the container - the nearly empty container - of coolant found in your barn."

"I remember now how my fingerprints would've gotten on that container. I went to find Jacob after a visit from Camille. She'd yelled at me and then said she'd wait for Jacob in the barn, and if I was to see Jacob I was to tell him she was in the barn. When I heard her drive away some time later, I went into the barn and saw some things knocked off the shelves. I didn't want Jacob to know she'd messed things up, so I tidied everything up. I could well have picked up the container while I was tidying. I didn't read the labels of the things I picked up."

"That sounds reasonable," Ettie said.

Kelly stared hard at Mildred. "You'd better be telling the truth this time, Mrs. Esh."

"Detective," said Ettie, "it occurred to me that Dr. Mackelvanner's inquiries over Nehemiah gave Camille information about coolant being so deadly. Doesn't that make you think that what you and I suspected was right – that Camille did kill herself? And, for that matter, wouldn't Jacob normally have picked things up if he'd found them knocked over in the barn? Thus getting his prints on them? Maybe that had been Camille's intention."

"Is that what you think? You think she killed herself?" Mildred looked directly at Kelly. Jacob once again put a comforting arm around his stepmother's shoulder.

Kelly raised his eyebrows at Mildred. "It's a strong possibility. Knowing that she was only going to die soon anyway and the fact that she was so bitter about her father leaving Jacob the farm." Kelly raised his hands in the air. "I guess we'll have to leave that for the courts to decide."

CHAPTER 21

*E*ttie groaned. Things looked bad for Jacob and Mildred since they'd lied about Camille's will. Would the courts believe Jacob was innocent of killing his sister? If so, would Jacob and Mildred go to jail over the fake will?

When Crowley and Ettie's eyes met, he said, "Are you ready to go?"

Ettie nodded. She'd done as much as she could to help Jacob, and now it seemed as though everything was out of her hands. Kelly was the first to leave Mildred's house and then Crowley, Elsa-May, Ava, and Ettie said goodbye to Mildred and Jacob.

While the four of them were driving back to Elsa-May and Ettie's house in Crowley's car, Ettie mulled the whole thing over. There were the cups with Jacob's prints in her apartment; his prints weren't even on the bottle of poison. They'd found that Camille had been lying about feeling she was in danger from her brother, and Camille had paid someone to shoot into her apartment making it look like

SAMANTHA PRICE

there had been an attempt on her life. How could the police still be holding Jacob accountable? Surely it wouldn't go to trial.

"I'm certain Jacob's lawyer should be able to get him off now. They don't have much to build a case on," Crowley said.

"Yes, I was just going over everything in my head. The only thing they have against him now is some cups in Camille's house with his prints," Ettie said.

"And the will he and Mildred wrote," Elsa-May was quick to point out.

"But did she really kill herself?" Ava asked.

"That might be something we'll never know for sure," Crowley said.

"Turn the car around, Crowley!" Ettie shouted from the back seat.

Crowley hit the breaks and pulled the car off to the side of the road. "What is it?"

"Turn the car around. We're going to Camille's apartment," Ettie said.

Crowley turned his head to look at Ettie. "You know where it is?"

"Her address was on top of the paper with her phone records that Kelly gave me." After Ettie gave Crowley the address, he turned the car around.

"What do you hope to find?" Elsa-May asked.

"And how are we going to get in?" Ava added.

"Ava, don't all people around the age of forty have a tablet, computer, or a laptop computer, or something of the sort?"

"I guess if they're *Englisch* most of them do."

"Just tell us what you're getting at," Elsa-May blurted out.

"It occurred to me that if I were going to kill myself, I would find out the best way to do that."

"And you're thinking she would've used the Internet and researched ways to kill herself?" Crowley asked. "I like it."

"So, you're going to check the search history if we find a computer?" Ava said.

"Not me. One of you will have to do that," Ettie said. "I only know that there is a search history; I wouldn't know how to go about finding it."

"I'm surprised you know something like that in the first place, Ettie," Crowley said.

"I know a thing or two," Ettie said with a smile.

"How are we going to get in?" Ava asked again.

"I don't suppose you also have a key, do you, Ettie?" Crowley asked.

"We'll find a way when we get there," Ettie answered.

"Couldn't we get into trouble? Isn't it breaking and entering?" Ava asked.

Ettie shook her head. "It's hardly breaking and entering if the person who had the lease on the apartment is dead."

"I don't know what the landlord would say about that," Crowley said as he stopped the car outside Camille's apartment building.

"It's number four," Ettie said.

"I'll stay in the car. My leg needs to rest," Elsa-May said.

"Sorry, Elsa-May. We should've driven you home first," Ettie said.

"I'm okay, don't mind me. These leather seats are nice and soft. Just hurry up."

Crowley said, "There's a button on the side of your seat near the door. Push it to lay your seat back."

Elsa-May pushed the button and her seat tilted back. "Aaah, I just might go to sleep." Elsa-May closed her eyes.

When the others got out of the car, Crowley said, "You two keep your voices down. We don't want to draw attention to ourselves."

They found apartment number four just one flight up. Then they stood outside the door. Ava tried the window, but it was locked.

"You're not a detective anymore, so just pick the lock or something," Ettie said to Crowley as the three of them stood in front of the door.

"I was a detective, not a criminal," he whispered back.

"But how are we going to get in if you can't pick the lock?" Ettie asked.

"All right, I'll do it," Crowley said while reaching into his pocket. "But don't tell anybody I know how to do this."

A giggle escaped Ettie's lips. "I thought you would've learned a few skills at your age."

Crowley kneeled on one knee. "I did have a few associations with some dubious people before I got onto the Force."

The former detective poked two metal things into the keyhole. Ettie peered over his shoulder to see what he was doing. He pushed the first metal rod in and then held it steady as though it was holding a lever, while the other metal rod appeared to be pushing something down. They heard a 'click.'

"Got it," he said. He pushed the door open and looked back at them. "Don't make any loud noises and don't turn any lights on. We'll use the light from my phone, and that's all."

Once they were in, Crowley shut the door behind them, and without the light from the hallway they were in darkness until Crowley flicked a switch on his cell phone. After some minutes of looking through cupboards and drawers, Crowley found a laptop in the drawer of the nightstand.

"Don't touch it," Crowley said to them as he spread his arms to keep them back.

They stopped still and watched him.

Ettie was amazed to see Crowley remove plastic gloves from his pocket. He pulled them on and said, "Fingers crossed."

"Are you sure of what you're doing?" Ettie asked.

"Of course I know what I'm doing or I wouldn't be doing it." A few pushes of some buttons, and a long list came up on the screen. Crowley scrolled down. "And there we have it, as clear as day."

"What is it?" Ettie and Ava asked at the same time.

"Search histories on DNA evidence, what poisoning with ethylene glycol does and how to implicate someone in a murder."

"Really? It's all on there?" Ettie asked, more surprised than pleased.

Ava straightened up. "I would never have believed it."

"I'm afraid I'm going to have to call Kelly and tell him what we've found. I'll have to take this in as evidence."

"What you've found. You can keep us out of it," Ettie said. "And make sure he deputizes you first or something of the kind so you don't get into trouble."

"I think when he sees this he'll be glad to have it," Crowley said.

Ava said, "I wonder why the police didn't take the laptop with them when they came here?"

Crowley answered, "She was murdered, they thought. If she was a suspect then they would've taken all her devices with them." He raised the laptop in his hands. "And we'll easily be able to verify whether or not this was in her possession on the dates she looked up all those sites, judging by the times she accessed her emails or other things like that. The tech people can verify things like that."

"That looks like the power cord," Ava said, pointing to the cord on the floor.

"I'll take that too," Crowley said.

Ava picked it up and handed it to him.

Crowley said, "I'll take this directly to the station, and then I'll take you ladies home."

THE FOLLOWING WEEK, Elsa-May and Ettie went to visit Mildred after they heard the news that all charges against Jacob had been dropped.

"You must feel relieved now that Jacob's free," Elsa-May said.

Mildred smiled. "I do. And he's so relieved now. I'm grateful to the both of you, and your detective friend, for looking into things. Without your help Jacob would be facing trial for murder. And the nice detective said he was going to recommend that our offense be classed a misdemeanor, which he tells me is a good thing. We might have to pay a large fine, but I don't care. It seems such a little thing now that Jacob has been let off a murder charge."

"Nice detective? You're talking about Detective Kelly?" Elsa-May asked.

"*Jah*," Mildred answered.

"All's well that ends well," Ettie said. "Who would've even imagined that Camille would've killed herself and deliberately made it look like Jacob did it?" Ettie turned to Elsa-May. "Well, I'd better get you home so you can rest."

While the two elderly sisters waited down at the end of the driveway for the taxi, Ettie noticed the man next door, Bradshaw. From the distance she was to him, he looked to be the size of her thumb, but she could still see him standing with his feet apart and his hands on his hips, glaring at them.

Elsa-May turned to see what Ettie was staring at. "Ah, the neighbor you were telling me about?"

"*Jah*, that's the one."

"He doesn't look happy."

"He wouldn't be happy now that he knows they're not selling the farm," Ettie said.

After Ettie was silent for a while, Elsa-May asked, "What are you thinking about?"

"Do you think that Camille would buy a car if she was about to kill herself?"

"*Jah.* She had to live like killing herself was the last thing on her mind if her plan was going to work."

"I suppose you're right."

THE TWO ELDERLY sisters weren't home long when they heard a man's voice call out through their open front door.

Ettie knew right away that it was Detective Kelly. She let Elsa-May stay knitting while she walked to the door. "Come in, Detective."

She showed him to the living room and once he'd said hello to Elsa-May, he sat down and faced Ettie. "Mrs. Smith, I want to firstly congratulate you, and secondly apologize to you. I'm sorry for how I've acted toward you. The stress of the job makes me go a little crazy sometimes."

Ettie gave a little laugh.

He shook his head. "I didn't listen to you, and I should've. I would've been able to solve this thing a lot quicker if I hadn't been so focused on Jacob being guilty. I'm afraid my team is overworked and we immediately head to the most obvious leads. Anyway, my behavior toward you was unforgivable."

"Nothing's unforgiveable," Elsa-May said, looking over the top of her glasses at him.

"That's right." Ettie nodded. "I accept your apology."

"In a way, I regret getting you involved, and in another, I ask myself what would have happened if I hadn't," Kelly said.

Ettie swiped a hand in the air. "You would've figured it out. Anyway, we ended up thinking along the same lines about Camille."

He breathed out heavily. "It seemed too far fetched. Who would've thought the woman would've set her brother up like that and then killed herself?"

"She was a tortured girl," Elsa-May said.

Ettie nodded. "Yes, it's very sad."

Detective Kelly nodded. "Some criminals are born and others are made. Seems Camille's early history set her up for a life of violence against herself."

After everyone was silent for a while, Elsa-May suddenly spoke. "Ettie, make the detective some tea."

"Do you have coffee?" he asked.

Ettie frowned at him. "I've got green tea or lemon tea, Detective."

"Tea will be fine. You choose which one. I suppose I've had enough coffee today."

Ettie pushed herself to her feet. "I made some lovely brownies today, too."

The detective patted his stomach. "Just the tea thanks, Mrs. Smith."

When Ettie brought the tea items back on the tray, she set them on a low table in front of the detective. "How did your promotion go?"

He shook his head. "No good, but I do pride myself on the fact that I guessed that the mother cooked up the scheme about the will." He picked up some sugar and poured it into his tea. Once he stirred the tea, he brought it to his lips and took a sip. "Now, I hope you might consider being my contact in your Amish community."

Ettie frowned. "What do you mean? Nothing ever happens in our community."

He set his tea down on the table. "According to our records, quite a bit happens with you Amish people."

Ettie pulled her mouth to one side; she was caught in a hard place. She couldn't trust him like she'd trusted Crowley, but she did want to help people when they were in trouble.

He leaned forward. "Would you consider helping me in whatever way I ask?"

Ettie thought her answer through carefully. "Well, if you need me, and I'm still around, let me know."

"Good. I was hoping you'd say that, because I've got a little matter that I was hoping you'd help me with, but it's not exactly police business this time. It will please me enormously if you agree."

Elsa-May leaned forward. "What is it, Detective?"

A grin broke out on the detective's face. "Mrs. Smith, would you make me more of your sausage and egg casserole? Perhaps a muffin or two?"

Ettie heaved a sigh of relief and held her hand over her heart while Elsa-May giggled. "You had me worried for a minute," Ettie said.

"I'll make you that casserole – mine's much tastier than Ettie's," Elsa-May said.

Ettie opened her mouth at her sister. "Elsa-May!" Ettie then giggled and said, "That's most likely true, but I'll bake you some bread and it'll be the best you've ever tasted."

"Not that you're boastful or anything like that, Ettie," Elsa-May said with a crooked grin.

"Exactly. I'm not being boastful, just factual," Ettie said with a nod of her head.

"Thank you, and since you're my inspiration to eat healthier, Mrs. Smith, I'd be delighted to taste your bread." He looked at Elsa-May. "And your casserole." The detective picked up his tea and took another sip.

Ettie pushed herself to her feet.

The detective screwed up his nose. "Are you sure you don't have coffee?"

Ettie chortled. "I was just getting up to get you some."

While Ettie was in the kitchen listening to the low buzz of conversation coming from Elsa-May and Detective Kelly, she reflected on how blessed her life had been. She'd been married for years to a wonderful man before *Gott* had called him home, and she had many children and grandchildren. Then there was Mildred who'd had so many problems in her life. Camille really had lived a tortured life, which seemed unfair.

Sometimes Ettie got dissatisfied living with Elsa-May and her annoying ways, but now Ettie realized how blessed she really was. *Denke, Gott,* she said under her breath. There are always others worse off, she thought. Why do some people have it easier than others? *Ach, the mind of Gott, who knows it?*

Ettie carried a mug of coffee out to Detective Kelly, wondering what kind of inquiries he'd have her make next.

Thank you for reading Amish Murder.

THE NEXT BOOK IN THE SERIES

Book 3

Murder In The Amish Bakery

A recipe for disaster brews as Ettie stumbles upon another dead body. This time, the unfortunate victim lies sprawled on the floor of Ruth Fuller's famous bakery. All Ettie wanted was to 'rise' to the occasion and perfect her loaf, not to 'knead' into another murder mystery!

Ruth, desperate to find the killer, bakes up a wild theory about recipe thieves and bakery brawls, while the police stick to a simpler recipe, focusing on the cash reserve. Could there be a 'grain' of truth in Ruth's theory? And what of the Bible clenched in the dead man's grip?

Join Ettie as she 'rolls' up her sleeves to sift through the 'floury' details of this mystery. In the midst of 'crusty' suspects and half-baked theories, can she uncover the truth, and also... can she finally bake a decent bread?

In 'Murder in the Amish Bakery,' the suspense is

'bread-hot,' and the mystery will keep you 'toasting' till the very end.

ABOUT SAMANTHA PRICE

Samantha Price is a USA Today bestselling and Kindle All Stars author of Amish romance books and cozy mysteries. She was raised Brethren and has a deep affinity for the Amish way of life, which she has explored extensively with over a decade of research.
She is mother to two pampered rescue cats, and a very spoiled staffy with separation issues.

www.SamanthaPriceAuthor.com

ALL SAMANTHA PRICE'S BOOK SERIES

Find a downloadable series reading order list at:
www.SamanthaPriceAuthor.com

Amish Maids Trilogy

Amish Love Blooms

Amish Misfits

The Amish Bonnet Sisters

Amish Women of Pleasant Valley

Ettie Smith Amish Mysteries

Amish Secret Widows' Society

Expectant Amish Widows

Seven Amish Bachelors

Amish Foster Girls

Amish Brides

Amish Romance Secrets

Amish Christmas Books

Amish Wedding Season

ETTIE SMITH AMISH MYSTERIES

Book 1 Secrets Come Home
Book 2 Amish Murder
Book 3 Murder in the Amish Bakery
Book 4 Amish Murder Too Close
Book 5 Amish Quilt Shop Mystery
Book 6 Amish Baby Mystery
Book 7 Betrayed
Book 8 Amish False Witness
Book 9 Amish Barn Murders
Book 10 Amish Christmas Mystery
Book 11 The Amish Cat Caper
Book 12 Lost: Amish Mystery
Book 13 Amish Cover-Up
Book 14 The Last Word
Book 15 Old Promises
Book 16 Amish Mystery at Rose Cottage
Book 17 Plain Secrets
Book 18 Fear Thy Neighbor
Book 19 Amish Winter Murder Mystery

Book 20 Amish Scarecrow Murders

Book 21 Threadly Secret

Book 22 Sugar and Spite

Book 23 A Puzzling Amish Murder

Book 24 Amish Dead and Breakfast

Book 25 Amish Mishaps and Murder

Book 26 A Deadly Amish Betrayal

Book 27 Amish Buggy Murder

Made in United States
Cleveland, OH
16 March 2025